Who Murdered]

Diana Has The Last Word.

by Cate Bryant

© 2022

Table of Contents

Introduction 3
Chapter One – Before I Married Delves Broughton 8
Chapter Two – Arriving in Kenya 25
Chapter Three – Falling in Love with Joss 35
Chapter Four – The Politics of Joss 50
Chapter Five – Romantic Interludes 63
Chapter Six – Murder Most Foul 83
Chapter Seven - The Trial 107
Chapter Eight – The Gilbert Years 116
Chapter Nine – The Post-War Years 133
Chapter Ten – Making Sense of It 143
Chapter Eleven – Meeting Idina 154
Chapter Twelve - The Mau Mau Years 171
Chapter Thirteen – The Next Husband 177
Chapter Fourteen – Living at Soysambu 196
Chapter Fifteen - Independence 204
Chapter Sixteen – After Independence 211
Chapter Seventeen – The Twilight Years 224
Bibliography 238

Introduction

Diana Caldwell was born in 1913. She left England during the first years of the Second World War and settled in Kenya, where she lived until her death in 1987, aged 74 years. She was married four times, first to Vernon Motion, then Sir Jock Delves Broughton, followed by Gilbert Colvile and finally, to Lord Tom Delamere. However, she was most famous as the lover of Josslyn Hay, Lord Erroll, Hereditary High Constable of Scotland, Baron of Kilmarnock, who was murdered in January 1941 on a lonely road on the outskirts of Nairobi. After Diana died, the *Daily Telegraph* published an article entitled "Femme fatale takes murder secret to her grave".

Thirty-five years later, this manuscript is being published. It is an 'imagined' autobiography, entirely unauthorised. Much of its content is historically correct, but some is pure invention.

The murder of Lord Erroll has never been solved. It has been the subject of much speculation and everybody who lived in Kenya at the time had their own pet theory. The book *White Mischief* by James Fox, published in 1982, was the basis of the film *White Mischief* starring Jock Ackland, Charles Dance and the divine Greta Scacchi. This film made it clear that although acquitted, Sir Delves Broughton, the cuckolded husband, was the murderer.

Various other people have been suggested as the culprit. If anyone really did know the name of the murderer, they never kissed and told. Many believed that it was Diana herself, based mainly on the fact that she had once carelessly thrown out the comment, 'Everyone knows I did it'.

Alice de Janzé, later Alice de Trafford, was also a prime suspect because she had been the intermittent lover of Joss since 1919 in Paris. Unlike Joss's other conquests, she was not blonde, and she was about the same age as him. It was believed that Alice was peeved that Joss had chosen Diana over her. She had once attempted to murder her alpha male lover, Raymund de Trafford, and this was deemed proof that she had the nerve to fire a gun at a man who had rejected her. Even Gwladys Delamere was considered a suspect as she was probably one of Joss's lovers, and she might have wanted him back for herself.

An altogether different theory was that Joss was assassinated by the British Secret Services because he had once joined the British Union of Fascists. He had dangerous knowledge of secret talks of appeasement at the beginning of the Second World War. Some say that Winston Churchill ordered the assassination. Others thought that it was Lord Baden-Powell who died a few days before the murder. I looked closely at the evidence for this in the book by Errol Trzebinski, *The Life and Death of Lord Erroll.* I concur with the opinion that the murder of Lord Erroll was not sexual jealousy. However, I could never understand how someone who was so threatening to the British war effort that he had to be assassinated could be appointed Assistant Military Secretary and was in line for an important promotion at the time of his death.

Other less popular theories were that Joss was watching the Germans who ran the gun shop in Nairobi, and they had gotten rid of him. Alternatively, JC Carberry, June's husband, hired a Somali to kill him because he had had an affair with June.

I have read all the books, except the one by Leda Farrant, which I couldn't obtain. I have puzzled over the mystery, and then it came to me one day. A suspect who had not been previously touted. Most probably he, but perhaps she, with a strong motive, who would not have been considered in those blinkered colonial times.

I was also fascinated by the character of Diana, about whom not much has been written. Many women of that era, perhaps a little older than Diana, have been fêted, such as Idina Sackville, Beryl Markham, Alice de Janzé, Edwina Mountbatten, and Diana Mitford. I tried to understand the psychology of Diana and see inside the rather brittle self-possessed shell that she presented to the world. Perhaps the Diana that I have imagined is nothing like the real woman but I have attempted a more complex interpretation of her personality and life.

I travelled through dramas and witnessed tragedies.

I knew great love, passion and joy.

I knew hatred and despair.

To appreciate one, you must experience the other.

The wind blows you to the ground, you struggle to your feet,

and survive.

Only the strong survive.

I have drunk from the cup of life until the last drop.

Chapter One – Before I Married Delves Broughton

My life story includes the elements essential for an entertaining tale – murder, adultery, curses, rags to riches, remorse and redemption. Over the years, I have made a considerable effort to inculcate an air of mystery or, to coin a vile phrase, 'kept myself to myself'. I knew that, eventually, I would have to tell all. The urge for self-disclosure is never entirely withstood, so this account will be published thirty-five years after my death. In the twenty-first century, 2022, no one is likely to care who killed Lord Erroll or how I spent the rest of my life after his murder, but I want to set the record straight.

In my younger years, I had to fight against the prejudices and dislike of many people to the point where I had given up on being loved, or even liked, for myself. I didn't much like myself at times, but I was driven by a determination to succeed. I don't think anyone was more surprised than myself when I came out on top.

I have been writing my autobiography, mainly in the form of a journal, for many years, but this was a well-guarded secret. I kept it locked away in my escritoire and hid the key in a secret hidey-hole. Of course, Gilbert and Tom knew, but I never let them read it, and they respected my privacy. Over time I have revised the narrative with hindsight and information that came to light long after events. I left instructions that this manuscript should be released thirty-five years after my death. I was always disappointed that none of the well-known biographers had come knocking on my door to write about me as they did Karen Blixen, Denys Finch Hatton, Idina Sackville, Alice de Janzé, or Beryl Markham. Thus, I have written this account myself.

Many people in Kenya were convinced that it was me who had pulled the trigger and killed Joss Hay, the Lord of Erroll. Even my stepson, Hugh Delamere, was sure that I did it. The rumour was that I had realised I was going to be stuck with an impoverished womaniser. Others have stated that Joss had learned that I had been having affairs in the short time of our relationship, and we were quarrelling. I adopted an air of studied indifference in the face of such spiteful attacks. I did my best to carry this off and carelessly threw off comments such as, 'Of course, it was me!' The closely guarded truth was that I had been there, actually at the scene, when poor Joss had been shot in the head. I had carried a pistol in my purse, and we certainly had been quarrelling. But it wasn't me. Finally, I will reveal what happened on that fateful night. It was none of the suspects that have been previously touted.

I will state emphatically that it was not my loyal friend, Hugh Dickinson, where ever he was that night, and there was some confusion about that. It was not at the scene of the murder. For a long time, I had thought that Jock had been involved, and he died under a heavy cloud of suspicion and thanks to *White Mischief,* his guilt will go down in history. Alice de Janzé, later Alice de Trafford, certainly loved Joss but not to the extent of killing him for choosing me over her. If things had turned out differently and Joss hadn't been murdered, it is quite possible that he might have tired of me after three years of passion and finally settled for her. She was inordinately rich. Not even Joss could have managed to run through her fortune in the way he did Idina's and Mary's.

Other theories concerning the British Secret Service, which were supposed to have orchestrated an extensive collection of assassins and accomplices who converged on that lonely road in a military-style mission, are much too complicated and fanciful.

There was a political motive, and although Joss's passing enthusiasm for fascism was part of it, the killing was not specifically his association with the British Union of Fascists, his secret knowledge of royal family indiscretions, nor top-secret Government policies of appeasement that were the issue.

Until 1935, I had had a mildly interesting but certainly not a noteworthy life. I was always pleased to be photographed for *The Tatler* or *The Sketch*. I suppose I was a minor success in my own small orbit, but I had not secured a titled or wealthy husband, which was my aim. I thought my luck had changed in 1935 when I met Sir Jock Delves-Broughton at Jack Fielden's house in Tadcaster, the Yorkshire village where Samuel Smith beer is brewed. Of course, at that time, Jock was married to Vera, who had been his wife since 1913. He was rich and titled and many years older than me. He was born in 1883. However, he was such a vain man that his birth year in *Who's Who* was listed as 1888. Vanity was not his only character fault. He was known as unpopular, humourless, arrogant, two-faced, sour, sulky, and a name-dropper. He always struck a pose as if a bad smell was under his nose. By the time he killed himself, he was nothing but a pathetic mess, and the world became a better place without him.

At our first meeting, I was twenty-two, and he was fifty-two years old. I had worked extremely hard to be a minor social success. Although I was not a conventional or natural beauty, I had very large, pale-blue eyes, masses of permed dyed-blonde hair and an adequate figure. My features were considered a little coarse, and I was not quite tall or slim enough to have a striking figure. But I certainly knew how to make the best of myself, perfecting this art when I worked as a fashion model, I was all too conscious that my mother and older sister were more beautiful than me, I made a considerable effort with my clothes and jewels, was always impeccably turned out, with lips painted bright-red.

Before I settled for Jock, my sister and I spent a lot of time at the nightclub, the Blue Goose in Bruton Mews in central London, a well-known hunting ground for young women to find rich, titled men. I was athletic and worked hard to master various sports. I also had elocution lessons to speak in a cut-glass accent. I hunted with the Grafton in Warwickshire, could fly a plane and was well-acquainted with the racing crowd. I suppose I was drawn to this milieu as my father, Seymour Caldwell, had gone to Eton and then became nothing more than an inveterate gambler. My greatest success in a long and arduous social climb was that I had been reported in *The Tatler* as being involved in a group of aristocrats who were aviation enthusiasts and hobnobbed with the Austrian Vice-Chancellor, Prince Stahremberg, in Budapest. It was later suggested that my passing social acquaintance with him was part of my career as a Mata Hari spy, working for the British Secret Services! This was ridiculous. My giddy social spirals were far too mindless to be involved in top-level espionage.

I have been compared to Wallis Simpson, which I do *not* consider a compliment. She was fixated on mirrors which were placed all around her home, gazing at her own reflection while she was talking to people. They called her

Wallis through the Looking Glass. She was described as plain, quiet, unpretentious and unprepossessing, but was a personage with a certain presence, walking into a room and expecting to be curtsied to. She certainly had complete power over the Prince of Wales as I had over my third and fourth husbands, Gilbert and Tom. When the Prince married Mrs Simpson, it was said that he was sinking lower and lower in his taste for women. Joss's choice of Phyllis Filmer, his lover before me, had been questioned, and perhaps I was considered even lower down the ranks than her?

I liked men, and they usually liked me. Although, most women took an intense dislike to me. I knew that I was considered that thing which was the worst of all faults, 'common'. I was tough, and I was ambitious. I had long adored Diana Mitford and wished only that I might be like her, but alas, I was not born an 'Honourable', nor was I such a beauty or as intelligent and witty. She had left her husband, Bryan Guinness, who was famed as the richest and nicest man in England and taken up with the well-known philanderer, Oswald Mosley, who at the time had still been married and declared that he would never divorce his wife, Cimmie.

I had wondered at this bizarre decision. I could not grasp why anyone would be so politically minded and enraptured with a man that they would leave such a perfect husband. She seemed to have no fear of making herself *declassé*.

I focused only on my personal ascent in the world. I had absolutely no interest in politics and was only vaguely aware that in the pre-war years, there was a vogue amongst the aristocracy for embracing fascism, which was seen as the only alternative to communism. They were all afraid they might have to share their wealth with the common herd. The cynical left-wingers saw fascism as an ill-disguised variant of exploitative capitalism. They say that the Prince of Wales was in favour of fascism, and he visited Germany to meet Hitler and made a deal that if Germany won the war, he would be put back on the throne. There were also rumours that Wallis Simpson had passed on state secrets to the Nazis. I had no idea if that was true, but it was a rumour grumbling around London at the start of the war.

I had wondered at Diana Mitford's unwise life choices. Not that I hadn't made my own disastrous personal decisions. One particularly embarrassing and horrendous mistake was my first marriage to a playboy musician called Vernon Motion. I was under the impression that he was rich, and it seemed we were two of a kind because he was under a similar illusion about me. We had married each other for money and found out that we were both penniless. When we separated, I was pregnant with someone else but miscarried.

My second marriage to Jock was also ill-judged. Although he was titled, he was not nearly as wealthy as I had thought. If I had married Joss, I would have tied myself again to someone without financial resources. However, I did learn from my mistakes and rectified this situation with my third husband! Gilbert Colvile was probably the richest man in Africa at that time. He was also a decent chap, and most importantly, he adored me and treated me like a princess.

As my admiration for Diana Mitford waned, I became fixated on another tall, slim blonde beauty who was swanning around London - Beryl Markham, who had grown up in Kenya and was steeped in the ways of the black Africans. She was famous for moving as if she had wings on her ankles, which they said was because she had learned to hunt with the natives - barefoot in the jungle and over the African plains. As a child, she had trained a giraffe to be saddled and ridden. They also said that she had an ostrich that could pull a cart. She was classically beautiful and utterly bewitching. Although interestingly, not particularly photogenic. Her most famous love affair was with Prince Henry, the third son of the King, and she had also had a fling with the Prince of Wales.

I had met her once when I moved in aviation circles. She was, as everyone said, single-minded and ruthless. At that time, she was with Tom Campbell Black, who was a superb flyer, and they said he satisfied her desire for a father figure. In 1936 she had flown solo from Kenya to England, following Tom, who was working as a pilot for Lord Furness. She had only logged 127 hours of flying before setting out on that epic journey. There had been no special preparations, and along the way, she had had a few problems, including a cracked piston. After that, she attracted a lot of publicity and was pulled into the whirlpool of London's nightlife and danced at the Dorchester, the Savoy and the Ritz. Someone had introduced me to her at the Ritz, but it had been a fleeting, 'How do you do'. I was very impressed by her insouciant beauty, femininity and grace. She didn't come across as an action woman who performed daring feats.

When I met her, Gervase, her son, was three years old. On that visit, she had seen him as her former in-laws, the Markhams, did not try to block her access to her son. She had separated from her husband Mansfield Markham soon after she had given birth. There had been a lot of rumours circulating that Gervase was fathered by Prince Henry. Beryl had had to leave the baby in England and returned to Kenya alone and destitute. She was not lucky in the romantic stakes and had only just become seriously involved with another man who she adored, Denys Finch Hatton, the former lover of Karen Blixen, when he died tragically in a plane crash.

Beryl's life was intriguing, and I began to dream of a larger-than-life existence in Kenya when Jock told me he owned land out there. He had received it in the Soldier's Settlement after the First World War. At that time, Jock was the best on offer. He set me up in a cottage called the Garden House on his Doddington Park estate in Cheshire, and I lived there with my mother and sister. Jock's father was the 10th Baronet, and he owned three properties: Doddington Park in Cheshire, Broughton Hall in Staffordshire and a house in Mayfair. Jock entertained lavishly in his 18th-century family mansion at Doddington Park, a house designed by Samuel Wyatt in the tradition of the times. There was even a menagerie with a tame bear.

Jock had house parties in Cheshire every weekend. Train tickets were sent to his London guests, and a band from Ciro's was hired to play for them on the rail journey. He loved reporters from the *Tatler* and the *Sketch* to photograph guests as they walked up and down the gravel drive in front of his mansion. What other people thought of him was one of Jock's obsessions, but by the time he committed suicide, he was universally despised.

His wife Vera spent a lot of time away from him, probably due to his annoying character. Vera was adventurous and great friends with Lord Carnarvon, Lord Roseberry, Sir Brograve Beauchamp, and most importantly, her great friend Walter Guinness, who became Lord Moyne. She travelled to exotic places and went on safari.

Jock referred to me as 'my blonde'. He loved to tell the story of how he had met my mother when she was pregnant with me. There was something particularly creepy about this. Looking back, I take the view that he treated me as a favourite possession, but it was the way that it was in those days. The only way a woman could enjoy even a modicum of freedom was if she was extremely wealthy. I wanted to be rich, titled, married and aristocratic enough not to worry about public opinion.

I was not accepted by many of Jock's female friends. They would even refuse to attend a house party if I was to be present. Anyway, I continued my carefree life in London, going to the 400 Club, dancing with handsome, dashing young men, and drinking champagne.

In 1938 Jock's daughter, Rosamund, married Lord Lovat, one of the Catholic Highlander families. Of course, I was not invited to the wedding. Then, finally, in 1939, Jock's wife left him. Lord Moyne's wife had died, and Vera hoped that he might marry her. I know that this was a terrible blow to Jock, who was pathetically lonely and hated to be publicly rejected.

I did become vaguely aware of rumours that Jock was in money trouble, but I discounted these as merely envious grumblings. He certainly had all the trappings of wealth with his grand estate and other properties. I was bedazzled with his connections to the upper echelons of society.

Looking back, I should have paid more attention. I was somewhat naïve about wealth and status in those days. Finally, the truth came out. Jock had sold much of the Doddington land in the years before the war. He had put £1.5 million in his own pocket rather than channelling it back through the estate. By the time his son, Sir Evelyn, who was the same age as me, discovered the fraud, Jock had only about £50,000 left. I had thought that Jock's idea of going to Kenya to grow food for the war effort was a bit thin. I found out later that he was running away from the disgrace of being discovered by his son as a fraudster. Sir Evelyn had been forced to go to Court to prevent Jock from further ransacking the estate.

My own father died around this time, and my mother was hopeless with money. The war had changed everything, and many of the old crowd had got swallowed up into the forces, and London was not the fun place it had been. Even my adored Diana Mitford, now married to Tom Mosley, was put in Holloway Prison, interned for her outrageous political beliefs. Before the war, she had become one of Hitler's intimates, visiting Germany with her sister Unity. How my goddess had fallen!

At that time, Jock proposed. He wanted to travel to Kenya with the rather fatuous excuse of growing food to feed the troops. He made it sound like he was personally going to be working in the vegetable garden. I certainly didn't love Jock, but he was a handy backstop, and the lure of Africa was strong. I had been fascinated by the stories of the carefree lives of the wealthy exiles in Happy Valley. I felt that I was suited to a life pursuing uninhibited, sybaritic pleasure. Ironically, my arrival in Kenya and the events that followed ended those careless days of the Happy Valley aristocrats forever.

Jock and I left England in the summer of 1940. War had been declared in the autumn of the previous year. Jock told me that Kenya would be drawn into the conflict but hopefully not bombed. In October 1935, the Italian army had invaded Ethiopia, wanting to claim land for a new empire for Mussolini in the Horn of Africa. The Ethiopians had fought back with spears but were soon overcome by the Italians' advanced weaponry. Somaliland had already been ceded to the Italians by the British as part of a deal in the First World War. Thus, Kenya had more than eight hundred miles of her northern and eastern frontiers bordered by Italy, which was in the grip of determined fascism.

Tanganyika to the south was British-mandated land but inhabited by many Germans. They thought their land should be restored to Germany under the leadership of Adolf Hitler. The British solved the problem by rounding up the Germans, who were believed to be members of the Nazi party and interning them.

Jock and I travelled to South Africa by sea. There were no well-wishers who had come to see us off among the mosaic of waving hands when the ship departed. I was still not altogether sure that I wanted to marry Jock, and once we sailed away, I enjoyed myself strolling on the deck with an assortment of admirers. We gazed at glorious sunsets, and when darkness fell, leant over the rail and watched pale green phosphorescence shining and writhing on the sea's surface. Jock was such a dismal old man among this group of interesting men. I imagined the possibilities of glamorous, handsome, dashing young men from aristocratic families who were reputed to live in Kenya.

On the ship, I read bits of Karen Blixen's book, *Out of Africa*, which had been published three years before. I was not a serious reader, and I struggled with lyrical prose and artistic descriptions. Certain phrases struck me, and I even made notes in my journal. I particularly liked the description of the horizontal trees, not shaped like bows or cupolas. It was an iconic image - those flat-topped trees in Africa.

One night, while dining on the ship, Jock talked about how the Mosleys would spend the war in prison because of their political views. Jock seemed to take a sly pleasure in this event for some reason. His face was contorted with malice when he talked about it.

"It was Lord Moyne, you know. Vera's friend. He was the one who wrote to the authorities. He never forgave Diana for leaving his son, Bryan Guinness, and after Oswald was interned, he was determined that Diana should be put away as well."

I found Jock's triumphant spiteful smile at this outcome particularly disconcerting. I had so admired Diana when I was young. I had wondered how such a beautiful, intelligent and elegant woman ended up in Holloway Prison. She had been dobbed in by her spiteful ex-father-in-law, and also her sister Nancy. I suppose I should have been impressed by Jock's access to such inside information.

"I didn't know that Lord Moyne was the father of Bryan Guinness," I replied lightly, glancing downward at my plate so that Jock couldn't see my expression.

"Vera told me in strictest confidence," he went on.

"I suppose I don't count then," I said quietly. I was struck by the incestuous interconnectedness of the upper echelons of British society. I would have to make notes to memorise all the connections. I had grasped the fact that most social discourse was spurious gossip.

At that stage, Jock and I never socialised together. We went out separately. Even when we got to Capetown in South Africa, he went out to dinner with one of his old friends, Cockie Hoogterp, who had been Baroness Blixen in her previous marriage to Bror, who had previously been married to Karen Blixen. I was not invited. Cockie was reputed to be a great friend of the infamous and much divorced Idina. Idina was the undisputed Queen of Happy Valley. She had married Joss Hay as her third husband. They had moved to Kenya, where she had gained just over half of 2,500 acres in the Wanjohi Valley in her divorce settlement to Charles Gordon. I had known about her all my life as she was a famous socialite. She was a woman who was steeped in deep, romantic and deadly sin. Her daughter, Diana, was born in 1926 in Kenya. I wondered what it must be like to be the child of such a famous much-married, and much-divorced woman. My own mother had had a 'reputation'. She had married my father reluctantly as she was pregnant, and he was much older than her. Later she had indulged in a *ménage à trois*.

Jock was such a name-dropper and impervious to any pique I might have suffered not having been invited to his lunch with Cockie. He took great delight in telling me about her friendship with Laura Corrigan. Laura had started out in life as a waitress and had unapologetically clambered up the social scale to be 'America's Salon Queen'. She was famous for her dinner parties prepared by the best chef in London when guests would be presented with gold cigarette cases or diamond watches. She had effectively purchased herself a place in high society. She was famous for her malapropisms. She often boasted of cruising on Vincent Astor's luxury yacht in the Caribbean. She had been living in Kenya in the 1930s. In early 1933 she went bush on safari with a retinue of famous people, including Vicomte de la Rochefoucauld, Count and Countess Paul Munster, two white hunters, a French maid and Cockie. At that time, Cockie sometimes acted as Laura's social secretary.

Jock had to work hard to persuade me to marry him. Finally, he proposed what he described as a pact. This term was a bit of a misnomer as it was more like an incentive package. The terms of the deal were that if I were to fall in love with a younger man, he would not stand in the way of me divorcing him, and he would provide me with £5000 per year for seven years after the divorce. In hindsight, it is doubtful that Jock could have afforded to pay me £35,000, but at the time, I was happily oblivious of his impecunious state. The terms of the pact were written up in a legal document by a solicitor and given to me before we married on 5th November 1940 in Durban.

Chapter Two – Arriving in Kenya

We travelled from South Africa to Mombasa by flying boat. On the same flight was John Carberry, called JC by everybody. He was notorious, not only very rich and mad keen on flying, but also a cruel, sadistic and twisted man. He hated the British and adored the American culture, notably the gangsters. He was famous for supporting the Germans in the war. Although he loved the hooliganism and random brutal violence of the bullyboy Nazis, it was unlikely that he would have enjoyed living in submission to the authoritarian regime. You could say he got his just desserts when the Kenyan army later destroyed his airstrip and confiscated his planes and yacht for the war effort.

Perhaps JC's upbringing in the creepy Castle Freke in Ireland laid the foundation for his vicious nature. This ancient castle had a history of feuds, hatreds, intricate plots, hobgoblins and foul fiends. JC was infamous for his cruelty to animals and fascination with killing as a child. Such a propensity for violence was perhaps a hereditary disorder. He had once described to his wife, June, that before he lost his temper, he would hear chattering noises in his head, which resembled something between the rattling clatter of cutlery in a drawer and the noises that a nest of baby crows uttered.

June was waiting at Mombasa airport, and we struck up an instant friendship. Having a girlfriend was a novel experience for me. June was great fun, and I began to enjoy the frivolous delights of a female companion. June was generally considered to be dreadfully common and dumb. She had scored herself a wealthy husband but had to drink a great deal of brandy to survive living with him.

Mombasa was beguiling. Waves were breaking and rolling across the sand banks. I could see strange-shaped trees swaying beyond the beach. Above the shoreline, the lush tropical vegetation, with its climbing carpet of flowering bougainvillaea, was charmingly offset with rows of white lime-washed houses with storybook-red roofs sitting amongst coconut palms. Natives dressed in vibrant colours clustered on the dock beside us. I was fascinated by the alien sounds of this exotic town with its population of Arabs, Africans and Europeans.

We stayed one night at the Manor Hotel in the old port. It was built in the pioneering days at the turn of the century and had a green-washed corrugated iron roof. Overlooking this part of the harbour was the pink Moorish fortress of Fort Jesus, built at the end of the sixteenth century. Now, it was a prison run by the British. Next to the fort was the exclusive Mombasa Club which had a seawater swimming pool. Old-fashioned majestic dhows could be seen from the terrace outside our room, sailing beyond the reef. They had once carried slaves to the Arabian Peninsula.

June entertained me with accounts of what the more happy-go-lucky Kenyans got up to. For example, it was the fashion that dinner should be served at eleven o'clock at night, and guests would wear lavish pyjamas and dressing gowns. King George V had taken a dim view of such slovenly habits and had instructed the governor, Sir Edward Griggs, never to allow such behaviour when he was dining.

After settling into our rooms and freshening up, we walked through the port, catching glimpses of the cargoes that came from the Arabian Gulf; Persian carpets, carved Arab chests, Indian roof tiles, sacks of Egyptian cottonseed, dried fruit, and piles of dried and salted fish. The mixture of pungent odours was so foreign that I felt I had been transported into an exotic world, a long way from dismal England. I was fascinated by the women clothed in *bui-bui,* voluminous black robes with only slits for their eyes. Native women wore next to nothing, just a bunch of rags around their waists, with large objects balanced on banana fibre rings set like halos on their shaven heads.

From Mombasa, we travelled by train to Nairobi. My stalwart supporter and loyal friend, Hugh Dickinson, 'Hughsie Daisy', had travelled to Kenya to be with me and was waiting on the platform. My relationship with Hugh was usually platonic. We considered ourselves like brother and sister. He adored me, and I trusted him. Although he was married, he had requested to be posted to the Signal Corps in Nairobi so that he could be near me. I gave him the legal document concerning the pact at that meeting, and he promised to safeguard it.

Many years later, I was to discover things about Hugh that I had not known at the time. He had been in cahoots with Jock in several fraudulent insurance scams. Perhaps, if I had known then, I would have realised that Jock's financial circumstances were shaky. Jock and Hugh had conspired to steal my pearls from the glovebox of a car when we were staying in the south of France. Then Hugh stole three valuable, insured paintings from Doddington Hall at the behest of Jock. When we arrived in Nairobi, I did not know about these ridiculous petty frauds.

We travelled in a box-body car from the station through the long dusty tree-lined streets to the Muthaiga Club, where we were to stay while we looked for a house. I gazed at the buildings that we passed. There was a medley of fine stone structures in the colonial style, interspersed with corrugated iron sheds, houses and shops that seemed flung down upon the streets without design or forethought. I gazed at a taxidermy shop with interest, which also sold various hunting equipment. The native quarters were lively, with crowds of people shuffling through the dust, wearing bright clothing and children darting from here to there. I longed to stop and peep inside their roughly constructed abodes. I wanted to see how they lived, what they ate and where they slept.

"You know this place started as a railway yard when they were building the railway from Mombasa to Uganda," said Jock in a lecturing tone.

"How fascinating," I replied sarcastically. The master and pupil thing which he practised annoyed me intensely.

On the day of our arrival, we had lunch and dinner with Gwladys Delamere at the Muthaiga Club. I liked the décor of this bastion of the white settlers. It was chintzy with a charming faded grandeur, buzzing with uniformed officers travelling between England and Cairo or up from South Africa on recreation leave. I could feel the ripples of admiring attention directed at me, and I revelled in it.

Gwladys was an old friend of Jock's. Her first husband had been Sir Charles Markham (the elder brother of Mansfield Markham, who had been so unhappily married to Beryl). They had had three children and divorced. She then married Lord Delamere, known universally as Dee, the great pioneer settler of Kenya. Dee had been twenty-seven years her senior and, by all accounts, had absolutely adored her. She was striking with pale skin, a huge head of bushy black hair, dark eyes, vivacious, intelligent and highly strung. Jock had told me that she was a colourful, hospitable person with a comprehensive collection of friends. She loved to mix different types of people, and although she could be aggressive, she would then dispel the tension with a deep throaty chuckle and an unexpected turn of phrase.

One of Gwladys's claims to fame was that when the Prince of Wales had visited Kenya, she had bombarded him with bread rolls at a Muthaiga dinner. Then she had rushed at him, overturning his chair, and they had rolled around on the ground together. Such rough-housing was not unknown at the Muthaiga with its reputation for public school boy shenanigans.

By the time I met her, she had been a widow for about nine years. She was now the Mayor of Nairobi and submerged herself in good works. I knew her approval would go a long way toward smoothing my social path in Kenya.

I also met Jack Soames at these welcome events. He had been at Eton with Jock. Jack was creepy. His wife, Nina, was emaciated and looked as if an unhappy spirit haunted her. I had expected to meet more exciting socialites than this and was somewhat disappointed. We set off up-country so that I might meet other old friends of Jock, including Lord Francis Scott, Mervyn Ridley, and 'Boy' and Paula Long.

I had high hopes of the Longs. I knew about Paula, whose maiden name had been Gellibrand. She had been a famous society model, described by her contemporaries as the most beautiful woman in Europe. She was one of the artistic, bohemian Bright Young Things who had cut a swathe through London in the 1920s. Cecil Beaton had loved her Modigliani features and slender hands - one of his favourite models. She had been close friends with Edwina Mountbatten and also Alice de Janzé. They had all shared a love of haute couture.

Paula's first husband was the Marquis de Casa Maury, usually called Bobby or 'The Cuban Heel'. He was a Bugatti driving Grand Prix winner who lost his fortune during the Wall Street crash and made it again running the Curzon cinema in London. They divorced, and he married Freda Dudley Ward, the most famous of the Prince of Wales's mistresses. Paula next married William Allen, but that marriage was only to last a year.

In 1937 she moved to Kenya. Shortly afterwards, she was at Idina's house, Clouds, and was introduced to Boy Long, an extremely handsome rancher who had previously worked for Lord Delamere. He was famous for his swashbuckling, flamboyant style of dress, wearing Stetson hats and Somali shawls, either tomato-red or electric blue.

When Boy had met Paula, he had still been married to Genessie. They had been core members of the Happy Valley set. Genessie was slim, elegant, adventure-seeking, and extremely rich like many of the Happy Valley wives. She was also known for her melodramatic temperament. The marriage between Genessie and Boy was dissolved in 1938. Genessie had then married Lord Claud Hamilton, a handsome Guards officer. Boy and Paula had married. They were a very striking pair. They lived up at Elmenteita, farming cattle. The Longs were older than me but much more fun than the ghastly old pervert Soames.

Jack and Nina Soames lived on a farm called Bugaret about sixty miles away. We drove over the Aberdares, known as the White Highlands, to the Nanyuki area. His farm was right on the equator. From his house, we could see the glittering snow peaks of Mt Kenya rising into the dome of the sky. It was about eight thousand feet above sea level here, and the air was light and invigorating, fizzing like good champagne. It has been said that the quality of the air contributed to the wild antics of the Happy Valley crowd. The winds blew from the northeast. The colours were a limitless range of ochre, brown, taupe and faded green, with red anthills spiralling out of the dust. Grey stone was scattered on the ridges. Karen Blixen described this landscape as the colour of pottery. What fascinated me was the blue-blue sky with huge floating clouds, billowing, white and ever-changing shapes. We saw herds of buffalo and eland. I took photographs. The wide, welcoming arms of Africa stretched out around me. A land that had been there for hundreds of years waiting for me. It was strange to have a deeply personal response to a landscape. I felt the mystery of Africa seeping into my being. I was discovering previously unknown depths to my soul.

I didn't let the rush of emotion show. I lounged in my chair like a film star, keeping up my *femme fatale* image. There wasn't much to do, and after a barbecue, we had a shooting practice that was to go down in history and become a focal point of Jock's trial. I was finding it hard to constantly be in Jock's company after the freedom I had enjoyed in England. To his chagrin, it turned out that I was a better shot and managed to hit the targets more accurately than him.

June had warned me about Jack Soames. It was well-known that he was a voyeur. It was said that he had drilled holes in the ceilings of the bedrooms in his house so that he might climb around the rafters and spy on his copulating guests. Jock seemed unaware of this abhorrent behaviour and told me that Soames had helped the Russians build tanks in the past, and now he was in charge of tank production at the railway workshops.

The arid plains spread out below the farm, and I stood on the veranda that evening gazing into the distance. Dusk was only momentary up here on the equator. One minute it was day with the pungent smell of dust and gum trees, and then the sun slid rapidly in a red-gold descent below the horizon. African black velvety nights were exotic, with the smell of night jasmine and woodsmoke, sounds of cackling hyenas, giraffes barking, the cough of lions and the rasping of crickets.

Chapter Three – Falling in Love with Joss

We returned to Nairobi on 25th November, and thank goodness Jock decided to go away for a few days. On 30th November, I met the man who was to tilt me on my axis and cause me to fall desperately in love for the first time. This strange, wild, unfamiliar experience that I had dreamed might happen in Kenya was upon me.

I had been in my bedroom writing letters and came down the stairs. It was the night of the Caledonian Ball being held at Muthaiga. My attention was caught by the sight of Joss dressed in a kilt. His mesmerising light-blue eyes held my gaze. My legs grew weak, and bright tropical butterflies fluttered inside me. I had an airy sense of exhilaration, fear, and desire mixed in a heady cocktail. I was looking into the face of true passion.

Later, I remembered what had been said about Diana Guinness when she had fallen in love with Tom Mosley. Although Mosley was tied to his wife, Cimmie, and Diana recently married, she had described a deep-seated feeling so definite as to be a "knowledge" that they were meant for each other. Now, I understood how she had felt. Nothing in life is so certain as first falling in love and being so sure that the world would arrange itself around one's grand passion.

There was a sense of joyous revelry in the company of Joss and his bevvy of masculine friends. I could feel the giddiness in the air as witty and daring conversation ran like a river, splashing, dashing and flashing. I wanted to belong to this group of brilliant beings and spend my life in their company.

Years later, I understood better the instant attraction between Joss and myself, which ran deeper than merely an appreciation of our respective physical attractiveness. I mean, the world is teeming with good-looking people, and they cannot all fall in love with each other higgledy-piggledy. We shared similar types of relationships with our parents.

My father was seventeen years older than my mother, and I had always been his favourite. This probably accounted for my precocity. He had petted and fussed over me. I was his little princess. He had been a tactile man, and I would sit on his lap and purr like a kitten. I had learnt my womanly wiles on my father's knee.

Joss also had a close relationship with his mother, who had blatantly favoured him over his brother, Gilbert and his sister, Rosemary. Gilbert was always markedly less flamboyant than the good-looking Joss and grew up to be a very quiet and reliable family man. Joss's mother was an Edwardian who did not leave her children constantly in the charge of nannies. The three children often travelled with their parents and an entourage of servants. Until the age of four years, Joss's mother dressed him in white frocks and tied back his long blonde locks with ribbons. Before bedtime, he would go to her boudoir and watch as her maid dressed her in evening clothes. Joss would pass the hairpins as her long brown hair was brushed and piled on top of her head in an elaborate style of the times. She often washed his face with her sponge and soap, and he associated the smell of female soap with love. This established his enjoyment of intimate rituals that he carried into adulthood.

Joss spent his childhood all over Europe as his father served in many important diplomatic posts. The family traditions were also steeped in the Scottish culture, which centred around their ancestral home of Slains. Bram Stoker, the author of *Dracula,* was a visitor who often went to Slains. He is quoted as saying that the history of the Errolls was full of dark rituals, fertility cults and blood sacrifice, more than he could ever dream up in writing *Dracula.*

After I met with Joss and my headlong tumble into that altered state of consciousness of being in love, Jock returned to Nairobi. He did not comment on any change in my demeanour. I imagined that it was plain for all the world to see that I vibrated and thrummed with an extraordinary lightness of being. The routine of lunches and dinners at the club, croquet games, bridge, backgammon and tea parties continued. I would have felt as if I were living the life of an old biddy if the constant possibility of Joss's appearance had not quickened my pulse every minute of the day.

In the evenings, Joss and I escaped to Ewart Grogan's Torr's Hotel to dance the night away, evading the dour presence of Jock. Grogan, nicknamed Grogs, could be seen encircled by female admirers. He was a handsome Irishman, tall and upright with penetrating blue eyes and dark arched eyebrows, producing an endless flow of chat. He was particularly voluble about the crass ineptitude of the government. He was most famous for his 1899 legendary walk from the Cape to Cairo to win his bride's hand, proving to her father that he was a worthy and resourceful man. In actual fact, his walk was from the northern tip of Lake Nyasa to Sobat on the upper Nile. Unfortunately, he was a swashbuckling buccaneer, and despite his heroic act to prove his worthiness, he went on to be shamelessly unfaithful to his wife.

One of Joss's and my favourite songs was the popular 'Let's Fall in Love', to which we danced endlessly. Our bodies melded together as we swayed sensuously to the music, oblivious of everyone around us. We felt as if we were the only two people in the world. We would often go on to the glamorous Claremont or the New Stanley Hotel and party into the small hours.

At this point in his life, Joss was single. His second wife, Mary Ramsay-Hill, had died just over a year before. Phyllis Filmer had been his mistress for the last couple of years. He was living at a cottage near Muthaiga as it was close to his work. When the war started, he had joined the Kenya Regiment as a Second Lieutenant, then promoted to Staff Captain. When I met him, he was Assistant Military Secretary.

He had married Mary on 8th February 1930 and had remained married to her until her death on 12th October 1939. They say that when Joss first met Mary and her former husband, he had fallen in love with their house, Oserian, nicknamed the Djinn Palace. His affair with Mary was carefully hidden from Idina, even though they had an open marriage. Mary had made sure that she wangled the house in her divorce to Ramsay-Hill. She had lots of money when she had married Joss, but by the time she died, her fortune was under £8,000 She had wanted to give Joss a son so much, but it didn't work out, and the despair pushed her over the edge. Hanging around with Kiki Preston, she had picked up a serious drug habit. Drinking and taking drugs excessively, there was no hope that she would survive. Joss was very patient and kind and humoured her until her death.

He had been seeing Phyllis for several years while Mary was house-bound and ailing, but his mistress was not included in many social events due to the loyalty of Mary's friends.

Jock struck up a friendship with Joss, and there was rarely a meal that the three of us didn't eat together at the club. Sometimes when I was elsewhere, Jock and Joss would still dine with each other. At one point, Jock went to stay at Joss's house for four days when I was not around. Jock was flattered at the attention of a younger man, and he entertained us with stories of racing, the London seasons and his experiences as a magistrate on the Nantwich bench. Joss's repartee consisted of caustic wit, unashamed self-revelation and bawdy innuendoes. I was also known for my love of *double entendres*.

When we had first arrived in Nairobi, we had formed the habit of horse riding every morning before breakfast. We hired mounts from Derek Erskine's Riverside stables, riding in the Kikuyu Reserve. Jock showed marginally more ability in the saddle than he did when shooting. There was still wildlife in those days on the edge of Nairobi. We passed flocks of Thomson's gazelles. Sometimes, an ostrich would emerge out of a clump of grass and run before us, black feathers gleaming in the early morning sunlight. Everything was fresh at this early hour before the dust rose and shimmered into the air and hanging in a haze throughout the day.

Now, Joss would join us. He was, as one would have expected, an expert horseman. As a child, he had lived in Vienna for several years and often watched the Spanish Riding School performances, so he was knowledgeable about *haute école* and *dressage,* the fine art of training horses. He had also been riding to hounds since he was seven, going out with the Marquess of Exeter's pack. Jock must have felt hopelessly outclassed when it came to horsemanship, and he complained about pains in his leg and stopped coming out with us. We were happy that it was just the two of us, and Joss entertained me with accounts of the polo matches that he had played over the years. He described the private race meetings and gymkhanas held by Major and Mrs Baynes on their estate near Nanyuki. Afterwards, there would be a dinner at the Silverbeck Hotel and dancing to Appleby's band. It sounded great fun, and I hoped we would soon settle into such a life. Being Jock's wife, even if we didn't share a bed, stretched my nerves to breaking point. All I wanted was to get away from him.

In early December, Jock and I moved to a rented house in the suburb of Karen on the outskirts of Nairobi. It was a Tudor structure with twenty-two acres of grounds, originally built by a Swiss couple who had been devoted to chamber music. We had fifteen servants, and I could hardly complain that we were living in a style to which I was not accustomed. Certainly, British pounds stretched much further in sunny Kenya than they had in dismal wartime England.

There was a small circular swimming pool, and I loved to skinny dip. I suppose there was an element of the exhibitionist in me, and much has been made of Jock's remark to Joss on one occasion when I was enjoying a refreshing swim, "Joss! It is my turn to dry Diana today." I continued to enjoy being seen in the arms of other attractive men. I was out and about with Hugh Dickinson and another new acquaintance, Dickie Pembroke, an army major.

On 22nd December, I was able to meet most of the Happy Valley people at a joint birthday party for Gwladys and myself. Although my name has been inextricably bound up with the Happy Valley set, it is worth noting that I was never actually one of them. I certainly never lived in the Wanjohi Valley, and most of the surviving members, who were in various states of decay at that point, did not want anything to do with me.

At the party in 1940, I was not deemed *persona non grata*. There were forty-four guests, and I was pleased to be a guest of honour, even if I shared the honour with the redoubtable Gwladys. The experience was even more piquant as many of

Joss's old girlfriends were present. Amazingly, he had once enjoyed a liaison with Gwladys. I was surprised by this as she seemed a rather strange woman, with her pale face and wild hair. June had whispered to me that she was going through the change of life and was becoming more and more unbalanced.

Idina was at the party. She had been Joss's first wife, although he was her third husband. They had a daughter called Diana, nicknamed Dinan. Now, Idina was up to her fifth husband, a flyer called Vincent Soltau, nicknamed Lynx. He was currently posted to Cairo. They had met when he had been at the RAF base in Mombasa. Idina was living up in the mountains at her house, Clouds, where she had a magnificent herd of Guernsey dairy cows. She would regularly come down to Muthaiga to socialise at the weekends.

Alice de Janzé, now Alice de Trafford, was also in attendance. At that time, I don't think she realised how Joss and my relationship would develop. When that became apparent, it was well known that she hated me with a passion. I found her life as fascinating as Idina's. I was mixing in a crowd of women who had been the most famous of their generation. They had earned themselves wicked reputations but lived life to the full, satiating themselves in pleasure and not sticking to the rules of decorum that society liked to impose on us. It struck me that I was younger than them, the next generation. I doubted I could make my mark in the same way that they had. But perhaps Joss would find in me everything that he had been looking for in his sampling of hosts of women before me. I was certainly younger than him. Previously, he had gone for women much older than himself.

Alice was famous for having shot her lover Raymund de Trafford at the Gare du Nord in Paris after he had rejected her. She had then shot herself. They had both survived, but she had been tried for attempted murder and got away with it. Even then, she had not woken from her Titania-trance until she had actually married Raymund and finally discovered that he was a very unpleasant man. He had been deported from Kenya a year before Jock, and I had arrived.

I remember very clearly a conversation I had with Alice at that party.

"What do you think of Joss being a fascist?" she asked.

I had looked at her in astonishment. Joss and I had never discussed politics. I had no idea that he was a fascist.

"But he is in the Kenyan army. They're on the side of the British?" I said hesitantly. Was Alice suggesting that Joss was on the side of the Germans?

"But he joined the British Union of Fascists years ago. He's thick with Tom Mosley. You know that Tom and Cimmie were witnesses at his wedding to Idina at Kensington Registry Office?"

"No, I didn't know that," I replied, once more struck by the fact that I was ignorant of so much about these people's lives. I had a sudden and disturbing vision of Tom Mosley, a demon-like figure in a black shirt, breeches and boots, swaggering around theatrically with a bodyguard of tough young blackshirts. I imagined Joss with his lovely blonde hair and blue eyes, an example of perfect Nordic manhood, striding in the Leader's shadow, as the fascists called Mosley.

"Yes. It was rather upsetting for Idina. You know her sister's friend, Barbie, was the one that lured her first husband Euan away. Cimmie was best friends with Barbie."

"I didn't really understand why Idina left Euan Wallace," I replied, thanking my lucky stars that I could remember the surname of Idina's first husband. That was the one where she had had two sons and left them behind.

"Oh, yes. Poor Idina! You know she adored Euan, and it almost broke her heart. But she has a strong spirit. She was proud and went because he publicly humiliated her with Barbie."

"But she loved Joss?" I suggested. "Why did they break up?"

"The problem with Idina is that she feels she has to marry everyone she has ever fallen in love with," said Alice. "She is just one of those women who must be married but cannot stay married. I suppose it was the same with me, leaving the darling Frédéric for Raymund. I fell for Raymund hard, and he treated me so badly. No one else liked him. Also, Joss has expensive tastes, and he had spent most of Idina's money when he left her for that Molly."

I had to process all these revelations. She had given me some insight into the human side of these women. They were wealthy and came from good families, married into the aristocracy and looked down on me as a mere commoner, but they suffered as all human beings do.

"But I've heard that you and Joss?" I said hesitantly. The thought of Alice with Joss in the past, and perhaps even the very recent past, was a thorn in my flesh. Alice was well-known as an American heiress, so rich that she would need ten lifetimes to spend all her money.

"Oh, yes. We have all fallen for Joss along the way," tinkled Alice. "But Joss tires of women after three years. He says that it is a strain on his vitality. You know his second wife, Molly, or as she liked to be called, Mary, managed to wangle Oserian from her husband before leaving him for

Joss. Her husband had a penchant for pornography and a very valuable collection locked away. I'm sure he took that with him, although they say Mary considerably improved her sexual techniques by pandering to his exotic tastes. They say that she had the skills of a courtesan. Joss just adores that house. I'm sure that was a good part of his attraction to Mary."

There was something in the way that she said this. The suggestion was that Joss was a man who used women to gain material wealth. This made me uneasy when perhaps I should have been reassured. I had no money except for that troublesome £5,000 a year in the pact. Would Joss get over his current infatuation and look for someone else with a divine house to offer or a substantial bank account.

"Have you been to the Djinn Palace?" asked Alice, her large grey eyes blinking at me myopically.

"No, Joss was going to take me there soon," I replied. "I've heard it is the most amazing place, like a Spanish *castillo*. He wants to introduce me to Gilbert Colvile. I believe he is a cattle baron, an old Etonian like Joss."

A moment of silence fell. I thought this was a tremendous opportunity to ask questions about Idina and Mary, the two most significant women in Joss's past. I felt insecure about both of them. They had been wealthy, with so much to offer. I wasn't sure what question to ask. Then I realised the revelation that Joss was a fascist was perhaps the most pressing issue.

"When you say Joss was involved with the fascists, what exactly did you mean?"

Alice was so vague that I felt she might just float away on a grey cloud. I needed to pin her down.

"When he and Mary were in London in 1934," replied Alice, as if reciting a story. "You know Mussolini had much influenced Tom Mosley. Joss was getting more serious in those days. It wasn't all partying and playing poke the penis through a hole in the sheet. He wanted to promote the cause of Kenya. Tom charged him with spreading the fascist gospel in Kenya and the colonies. I think it was then that Tom gave Joss the vision that he might become the leader of Kenya."

For a moment, I forgot about the implications of fascism, pushed aside the troubling vision of Joss's penis waggling through a hole in a sheet, and thought of myself as the Countess of Erroll, the first lady of Kenya. It was a dazzling vision. Exaltation flashed through me. I wanted to talk to Alice all night, she had so much to tell me, but she floated away and stood next to Idina on the other side of the room. By the night's end, she had realised that Joss and I were in a serious relationship, that he intended to marry me. Alice then hated me with a passion. There was often speculation that she had killed Joss, but no one could understand her reasoning. Surely it would have been more logical to kill me. Alice believed in the afterlife. When the judge had asked her why she had shot her lover Raymund and herself at the Gare du Nord, she said that she wanted to be with him in the Great Beyond. I had had enough religious education at school to wonder whether Alice, Raymund, or even Joss would qualify to go to heaven. I felt it more likely that they would plummet like stones into the inferno.

Chapter Four – The Politics of Joss

I had never been interested in politics, but now I had an urgent need to understand fascism and, more importantly, the British Union of Fascists. I was wary of asking Joss himself. I thought that I might betray my utter ignorance. It was no good discussing it with June, although an avid gossip, she had no interest in serious matters. Perhaps, her husband might have been a good source of information. I understood that he was very pro-German, but he was away in South Africa.

There was a gentle old professor who lived in a cottage near Muthaiga, and the next day, fortuitously, I found myself alone with him on the club's veranda. Obviously, a professor would have political knowledge. I broached the subject and with barely a blink of surprise at this odd request, as if people asked him about all sorts of heavy subjects every day, he explained it to me patiently and clearly.

A fascist movement began in England in the 1930s. At that time, British fascism was more generally prevalent, not as inextricably bound up with the Third Reich as it is now. It began with sympathy for Germany's harsh treatment at the end of World War I with the Treaty of Versailles. Hitler had come to power at the beginning of 1933, and Germany was getting back on its feet after suffering such a terrible defeat.

There were new houses being built, social welfare programmes and visitors coming back to England talking about the lowering of unemployment and a mood of optimism. The Depression still had a grip on England, and huge unemployment prevailed. One per cent of the population in Germany was Jewish, and there was a wide distrust in Europe of the Jewish grip on the financial institutions. Many upper-class British were linked by blood and marriage to Germany, and there was a general appreciation of their culture. This was most notable with the Royal family, who was more German than British.

In 1934 Lord Rothermere, owner of the *Daily Mail*, had given his enthusiastic support for the British Union of Fascists and such headlines as "Hurrah for the Blackshirts!" and "Give the Blackshirts a Helping Hand" were emblazoned across the front pages. Mosley was making stirring speeches about glorious patriotism and the expansion of trade within the Empire.

The British Empire was important to Joss, which attracted him to this creed. He was keenly interested in promoting the cause of Kenya and raising its level of prosperity. By all accounts, Tom Mosley was a persuasive, dynamic figure and practised philanderer who seduced women more successfully than Joss. Tom and Joss were quite similar in character, although Joss was more flippant and less intense.

I knew that Hitler was famed for theatricality, militaristic pomp and ceremony, uniforms and symbols. Mosley used the same sort of techniques. But I could not imagine Joss indulging in that sort of pantomime. After Joss's conversion to the creed of fascism, he returned to Kenya. He had already served as Chairman of a District Council for three years, Chairman of the Convention of Associations, and Secretary to the elected Members Organisation. Then, he was elected as MP for Kiambu, Ruiru and Limuru. He was sworn into Kenya's Legislative Council, which at that time consisted of eleven European elected members, four Indian elected members, one member to represent the Arabs and two unofficial nominated members, both white, representing the interests of the native African community.

At the time, like most of the white population in Kenya, it did not strike me as unfair that the native Africans should have no elected representation. It never occurred to us that the white Europeans should not be in charge. It was the great British Empire. Such a terrible miscalculation! But our thinking was shaped by the underlying unquestioned beliefs of the times. We were imperial settlers who were utterly convinced that we should be the natural rulers of Kenya and that black Africans were merely feudal subjects.

Racial segregation was embedded into the colony's structure, and Africans were considered a resource to be exploited. There was no question that they should have rights equal to those of the European settlers. In 1932 there was a Land Commission to judge native Africans' claims against the government and white settlers, defining the boundaries of the White Highlands. The Commission rejected the idea that the Kikuyu had lost land through alienation. They refused to recognise *githaka* land title and ruled that squatter settlement on white farms would never mean legal title. From 1937 the law said that squatters were labourers, not tenants and local councils had the right to regulate native stock and labour.

Tentatively, I asked the professor about Joss and the way he had promoted fascism in Kenya. He looked at me sharply. The afternoon sunlight filtered through the vine that hung from the veranda eaves. It was such a warm, somnolent afternoon that grave political matters seemed out of place. The boy brought us more cool drinks. The professor looked to the right and left to ensure we were not being overheard and began another explanation.

He told me that I had to understand the way things are in Kenya. Sir Francis Scott and Joss firmly believed that the country should have self-government by whites, as had Lord Delamere and many others. During the Grigg regime, the white settlers had gained only a small influence in the government process. Decisions were made in Westminster, and decrees were issued from the Colonial Office in London. The people making these decisions rarely visited Africa, and the white settlers were constantly up in arms over the petty-fogging and ridiculous rules and regulations. So, it made sense that the two groups didn't get on. The settlers arrived intending to make Kenya their permanent home. They were in it for the long haul. The local officials were here as representatives of the British government merely to serve their terms and work towards their pensions. They would retire and return to England. They did not have the same emotional investment.

Then, Joss converted to fascism when he and Mary were in England in 1934. He returned to Kenya a fully-fledged fascist. He made his conversion public in an address as the Chieftain of Nakuru's Caledonian Society in the presence of Governor Byrne. He made some damning comments about the British Government and how the parlous state of Kenya's economy had been ignored in the recent budget. This speech made headlines in the *East African Standard*, 'Earl of Erroll's Outstanding Criticism'.

Shortly afterwards, at Njoro, Joss made another speech specifically about fascism. It was about super-loyalty to the crown, absolute religious and total freedom, an insulated British Empire, hardly any imports from foreign countries, higher wages, and lower living costs. Mary was heard telling people that within five years, Joss would be the dictator of Kenya.

In his next speech at the Rongai Valley Association, he made clear that British fascism was entirely different to the Nazi movement in Germany. He presented it as a pure form of nationalism and loyalty to the British Empire.

In the following year, Joss was pushing for the Morris Carter Land Commission's recommendations about the Aberdares being officially declared the White Highlands for the exclusive occupation of Europeans beyond the boundaries of the local towns. The British government had delayed this because of the claims of the Indians in Kenya and the worry that it might create unrest in India, where they were clamouring for independence.

However, things were changing here. Joss and Lord Delamere had both been keen that Tanganyika be united under the umbrella of the British Empire but well-governed rather than under the direct authority of the British government in London. Lord Delamere had died, and with the Second World War on the horizon, Oswald Mosley's fascists were calling for Tanganyika and southern Kenya to be returned to Germany. At that point, Joss promptly withdrew his support for the British Union of Fascists.

I had begun to understand the way things were organised. There was a difference of opinion between the British

Government and the Colonial Office, and the white settlers. This encompassed the rights of the black Africans, and it all boiled down to land ownership. I never questioned the justice of colonialism and how white Europeans came to Africa and carved it up as their God-given right. But, when you thought about it, one could see that the blacks might have a greater claim than this alien order that had been imposed on them.

From a personal perspective, I liked the idea of Joss being an MP, a leader of Kenya, with me by his side as the Countess. I had never really considered a role in public life. In the past, I had focused on social status, sexual adventure and living a life of luxury. I thought about how Edwina Mountbatten, who had previously spent her days and nights indulging in steamy affairs and travelling to exotic lands, had stepped into public life in 1938 with the war looming on the horizon. She had been galvanised into action and decided to do something useful for a change. She was half Jewish and, besides training with the Red Cross, became an advocate for the refugees streaming into Britain. She was on various refugee committees and wrote letters to the British authorities.

Then, she was appointed Lady County President of the Nursing Division of the London Red Cross and the Order of St John, responsible for all St John Ambulance volunteers working in Rest Centres, Shelters, and First Aid Posts. Every night she toured around the streets of London, inspecting each shelter. She had had her uniforms specially tailored with shorter skirts and tight-fitting jackets and wore her hat at a jaunty angle. She exhibited a gift for leadership and organisation and used her connections ruthlessly to do good.

I thought I might do very well at this type of work. I could certainly present a glamorous but workmanlike image, and as the Countess of Erroll, I could swan around and be seen as doing good on the world stage.

I came out of this happy daydream, and my thoughts returned to Kenya's problems. Like other white people then, I had no idea what was coming within the next twenty years. We were all happily oblivious, so sure that we were superior beings and could walk the earth and claim all the good things for ourselves. The issue was land, who owned the land, and who had the rights to the land. Joss was firmly of the belief that there should be settler self-government. He was determined to resist any British Labour government attempts to assert native rights.

Joss had always been interested in the intricacies of world trade, and he had chafed against the restrictions of the mandate system and the Congo Basin Treaty. Mosley's idea of an integrated trade system throughout the British Empire would have appealed to Joss. I think this underlined his patriotism. He was not aligning himself with Mussolini or Hitler but rather looking for a way to advance the interests of the British Empire. I doubt he knew that Mussolini was financing the British Union of Fascists.

I thanked the professor for his lengthy explanation and went to my room to change for the evening. After dinner with Jock, Joss and I would slip away to dance. We were happily oblivious of the dagger looks directed at us when we clung to each other on the dance floor. There was an extraordinary magnetism between us, and it was impossible to hide our mutual attraction. I would have to steel my heart against these women who blatantly disliked me. They said I was a common gold-digger. I consoled myself that I was younger and more glamorous than them and still had all my chances.

Upon consideration, I found their self-righteous judgement unreasonable. Idina was famous for having left her first husband, the rich and handsome Euan Wallace and her two young sons. Then, she married a man called Charles Gordon, divorced him and married Joss. She was now up to husband number five. Alice had been married to a lovely, gentle, intellectual man, Frédéric de Janzé, a French count of impeccable breeding and had left him when she had fallen for the very bad man, Raymund de Trafford. Even Diana Mitford, who had been married to the richest and loveliest man, had run off when she had fallen in love with the philanderer Oswald Mosley who had told her that he would never leave his wife for her. I had to face the fact that it was not necessarily because Joss and I were in love, but rather that these women just didn't like me. Fortunately, I had June as a friend, as ditzy and drunk as she was. She was very supportive of my relationship with Joss.

The best times were when Joss and I were alone at his bungalow opposite the grounds of Muthaiga. It was small and unpretentious, but I didn't care. It made a perfect love nest. All signs of Mary, his dead wife, had been removed, and we could be together unobserved. Sometimes Lizzie Lezard, one of the old Etonians who was a close friend of Joss, stayed there but made himself scarce when I was around so we could be alone. We were waited on by Joss's devoted servant, Waiweru.

The wooden posts of the veranda were tangled with bands of honeysuckle and cherry-red, orange and purple bougainvillaea. We would curl up on a love seat and look over a velvet lawn with bright, curving flower beds. A wall of shrubs and flowering bushes, scarlet poinsettia and white frangipani around the garden's perimeter gave us privacy. Joss explained to me how the refractory table and eight chairs in the room where we dined were pieces of furniture that had been in his family for generations.

One night I took a deep breath and asked Joss about Mary. Usually, he was casual and insouciant when it came to personal matters, but that night, he opened up, confirming what I had already heard from June, Alice and the professor.

"Poor Mary was devastated that she couldn't give me a son. I repeatedly said that I didn't care, but it was a matter of pride for her. Being the Countess of Erroll was not enough. She wanted to produce an heir, to show the world. Kiki Preston, who died before her, was a bad influence. She supplied her with heroin and morphine and got her heavily addicted. Kiki lived next door to us at Oserian, she and her husband, Gerry. Kiki had unlimited funds, and in the early thirties, whenever her supply of drugs ran out, she sent a pilot to fly to Greswolde-Williams to fetch more."

"More recently, I got involved in politics and believed in the cause of making Kenya prosperous and a successful nation. I wanted to encourage tourism to bring in funds, particularly promoting Lake Naivasha. I can't wait to take you there. It is beautiful. Before the war, we had sailing regattas, and I've got the polo ponies. The situation with Mary got pretty grim. She became increasingly out of control and, in public, showed herself up badly. She was covered in sores and abscesses from the heroin use and would make malicious remarks in a loud voice. I just had to carry it off and hope it would not harm my political work. At home, she was very bad-tempered and bitter. I felt so sorry for her, but there was nothing I could do. I knew she was dying and tried to make it as easy for her as possible."

"She died in October, over a year ago, and it was at that time that war was declared. I'd been working in the Manpower office. It was quite complicated. We had to devise a plan, allocating men to different jobs when the war came. There were many roles to think about, not just soldiers to battalions but things like the ARP, Red Cross, fire-fighting, all sorts of side issues, and ways to organise farms and pay farm workers' salaries. Kenya was meant to be supplying food to the war effort not only in Africa, but also in the Middle East."

"I was racing all over the countryside with Arthur Clark, and there was a locust plague in the months before the war. Then twelve days after war broke out, our offices went up in smoke. All of the Kenya Secretariat was burnt to the ground."

"Thirty years of colonial administration destroyed in a few hours. All the Manpower records which I'd been working on were gone. Everything in the Lands Department was burnt, the leases, the allocation of land, the lot. They could never ascertain how the fire was started, but it was in my office."

"We had to put back together all the Manpower records, working from memory. They say I've got a photographic memory, and it certainly helped that I could remember details of people and the placements."

"You've got a photographic memory!" I exclaimed, thinking there was no end to this wonderful man's talents. It sounded like he had been a hero in these circumstances. Several years later, the significance of the fire emerged.

"You know it was after that fire that locusts which were swarming around the country arrived in Nairobi," he went on, ignoring my exclamation. "They ate all the lawn at Muthaiga. They left the worst smell behind them. It was a blow at a time just before the war started when we needed to be stockpiling food. I was starting work on the Agricultural Production and Settlement Board. Then there was the worst drought in living memory."

At this time, when we were discussing the world that Joss lived in, our relationship took on another dimension. I began to think about the way we would shape our lives together. I was determined to throw myself into Joss's work and support him, becoming knowledgeable and a sounding board. I was preparing myself to discard my frivolous ways and try to build a better life not just for us, and hopefully our children, but for the people of Kenya.

Chapter Five – Romantic Interludes

After Christmas and the New Year, June began to actively help us to escape so that we could be together. We went to her house Seremai, five miles from Nyeri. Joss's chauffeur, Noor Mohammed, drove us. It was utterly divine to have three days and two nights of blissful happiness together

It was a hundred miles from Nairobi to get there. I had mentioned Beryl Markham and found that both June and Joss had known her quite well. June told me that Beryl had spent Christmas with them a few years before, and they had flown to Kiki Preston's place. Of course, I had heard of Kiki, a beautiful and witty woman who openly used drugs, injecting herself publicly with her silver syringe. Joss had told me how she was the one who had got Mary into heroin.

June teased Joss about his dalliances with Beryl when he had been married to Idina, living at Slains. This had been when Idina had presided over the wild parties that had made Happy Valley infamous. Joss had smiled smugly, but neither confirmed, nor denied the accusation.

"I thought you only slept with married women," I said lightly, trying to carry it off as if I didn't care.

"Oh, Beryl was married. Her first marriage was at the age of sixteen. Her father virtually sold her to a man twice her age to cancel some debts. She ran away from him. He was a violent sod. Then later, she married Mansfield Markham. That was when she had an affair with Prince Henry, and they say she dallied with the Prince of Wales as well."

"Goodness!" I exclaimed. "I feel as if I'm a mere babe in the woods compared to you lot."

We drove up an arched tunnel of green-leafed trees. There was a line of grevillea on the outer edge of the avenue.

"Grevilleas are used to grow around coffee trees," Joss told me. "They have a lot of nectar that not only attracts bees, which pollinate the trees but also attracts very bright sunbirds."

I was dazzled by the brilliantly coloured tropical flowers and blooms that hung across every surface and clumped all over the ground. Purple bougainvillaea, more grevillea of every colour, a yellow-orange flowered vine, and bright red tulip-shaped flowers on flame trees. The coffee blossom gave off a scent of orange and white cream.

"What type of tree is that?" I asked in surprise.

"It's a monkey puzzle tree," chipped in June from the back seat. "But look over there! There are the tennis courts!"

"We must have a game," I said to Joss.

"Perhaps," he said and smiled at me in that way that suggested bedroom activities.

The house itself was no architectural marvel, certainly nothing like Doddington Hall. It was one-storey, grey stone, with sloping roofs made of wood shingles and tall chimneys. We went inside the house, and June led the way through to the inner courtyard. There were gorgeous lilies and oleander bushes, and doors to the guest rooms led off from a corridor that circled the courtyard. The drawing-room had a miraculously polished wooden floor and a huge fireplace. A grand piano stood in the corner.

"Of course, no one ever plays it," said June carelessly, gesturing towards the impressive musical instrument. She called to one of the boys beside the doorway and asked him to bring us drinks to the veranda.

We stood looking out across the views.

"You know the name Seremai is a Maasai word meaning 'place of death. It's called that because this was where a battle between a Kikuyu tribe and the Maasai took place."

Like a tour guide, Joss went on telling me that it was thirty miles south of the Equator. Because it was 5,000 feet above sea level, there were no mosquitoes, and we didn't have to sleep under nets. The evenings and mornings were cool, and there was no oppressive humidity.

The view from the house's veranda encompassed the twin peaks of Mount Kenya, which was thirty miles northeast, towering seventeen thousand feet above the surrounding landscape. This mountain was always capped with snow for at least three thousand feet, no matter how high the temperatures. To the left was Nyeri Hill, covered with dense green forest.

June gestured across the paddock to an airstrip and a hangar on the property.

"You know that Beryl Markham was up here all the time. My husband let his mechanic work on her planes, and she used to borrow his planes. She worked as a commercial pilot."

"I would love to meet her again. I was introduced once in London. I'm sure she would never remember me," I gushed. "I find her rather fascinating."

June shrugged nonchalantly.

"Our Beryl is not very interested in women. She gets on better with men. No taste for girly gossip. You know she never really had a mother. The only maternal influence was Lord Delamere's wife, Florence. When Beryl was young, Lady Delamere took an interest in her."

"Oh," I said. I must have looked a little hangdog.

"Darling, don't try and compete with Joss's old flames. He is talking about marrying you. That, in itself, is certainly an achievement."

"You know, there is something that worries me. Someone said I can't remember who, that even after I'm divorced, I won't be able to remarry for three years."

"Well, we'll just have to hope that Jock will kick the bucket," said June, giggling.

I laughed with her. That was certainly a scenario that would end this ghastly fiasco.

June was heading off to Malindi to give us some time alone. Joss and I waved goodbye to her and turned to each other. Looking into your lover's eyes makes you feel as if you are drowning in a pool of happiness, and all the complications of my husband, a divorce, and Joss's former conquests dissolved instantly.

That evening we sat on the veranda. We could see the *shambas* of the farm workers dotted across the hill below us. They had allotments that were terraced, and they grew corn ground up and made into their staple dish of *posho*—the feathery heads of the corn cobs rippled in the evening breeze.

"You know that there are two harvests a year in this country," said Joss proudly. I could tell he loved this land,

and I felt a rush of emotion. Not only were we magnetically attracted to each other sexually, but we shared a love of Kenya. The sing-song voices of the native women shimmered through the darkness.

I loved the idea of mixing with aristocracy and pressed Joss on his acquaintanceship with royalty. He told me about a sea journey he had taken with Mary when they were first married. They were travelling on the *Modasa,* sailing down the east coast of Africa from Beira to Mombasa. Edward, the Prince of Wales, was on board. Joss told me how they had a lot in common. The Prince adopted full Highland dress at dinner, including kilt, jabot, sporran, and *sgian dugh* tucked into his stocking. Joss had had the habit of changing into his kilt when he had breakfasted on porridge at Slains. On a more serious level, the Prince and he shared a hatred of war after the mass slaughter on the battlefields of World War One. They also agreed that the white settlers should govern the colonies, not the Colonial Office in London. Neither of them wished to see the blacks in charge after all the work the settlers had put into the land.

When they docked in Kenya after that journey together, they discovered that Lord Delamere had been running a campaign to promote the solidification of 'the white ideal' in Kenya, Tanganyika and other Central African countries. These views were not aligned with the idea of paramountcy that the Duke of Devonshire had declared at Whitehall. This idea was that the interests of the natives should always be paramount over the interests of the European settlers. Although, it was officially the view of the British government it was never enforced.

Joss humoured me with my patent admiration of his connections with famous people. He told me the charming story of how Lake Naivasha was the inspiration for the book *Babar sur l'Île des Oiseaux* by Jean de Brunhoff, who was the cousin of one of Joss's neighbours, Giselle Rocco. She and her husband, Mario had lived on the shores of the lake in a cluster of thatched *rondavels* rather than a European-styled house. Unfortunately, Mario was Italian and had been interned at the start of the war.

Joss clearly loved Oserian, and told me about all the sports that could be practised there, mainly due to his efforts after he and Mary had got together. There was tennis, squash, riding, polo, yachting and swimming either in the lake or the swimming pool. I told him it sounded like heaven. I loved sports.

He and Mary had entertained lavishly at Oserian. Then he had realised that he wanted something more from life than sybaritic entertainment, and in 1932 he had entered local politics, sponsored by Governor Byrne. One of the first issues that he got involved with was the introduction of income tax into Kenya. Joss and Major Cavendish-Bentinck were totally opposed to this idea that Whitehall and the Colonial Office were imposing. I had been tempted to ask him about the BUF, but I didn't want to look like I had been checking up on him. I didn't mention that I had already sought out information about his recent political career. I thought, in his own time, he would tell me the full story himself.

Our retreat from the world at Seremai passed swiftly, and then we drove back to Nairobi.

"What is wrong with the windows?" I asked. "It's hard to see out of them. They're all blurry."

"Oh, I had been driving past the Somali settlement a few months ago, and someone fired some shots at me. So, I had the windows replaced with bullet-proof glass."

"Gosh, I didn't realise that the black Africans were violent towards the whites," I exclaimed.

"Not usually. It was a one-off incident," he said dismissively, implying that he did not wish to discuss it.

Before we returned to Nairobi, he instructed the chauffeur to take us to the Eastleigh racecourse where the annual East African Derby was being run. He took me up to meet the Blin Stoyles in the members' enclosure. I knew that this was a sure sign of his commitment. He wasn't attempting to hide me away, and when we returned to Nairobi, I stayed with him at the bungalow for two nights, not bothering to return to the house in Karen.

Not everyone was pleased with our relationship. Someone had left a poisonous note in Jock's pigeon hole at the Club. It said:

You seemed like a cat on hot bricks last night. What about the eternal triangle? What are you going to do about it?

Jock showed me the note, and we laughed it off, but it meant that my husband could no longer ignore the signs of my passion for another man. Jock tried to make the best of it and brought up the subject of our planned trip to Ceylon later in the month. I made an excuse that I needed to work on the house.

I could feel the animosity from the old guard, what was left of the Happy Valley crowd. Their glory days of carefree hedonism were coming to an end anyway. They had frittered away their youth with pointless chatter, jokes and pleasure-seeking. Alice de Janzé's second marriage to Raymund de Trafford had been a disaster. Kiki Preston, who Evelyn Waugh had described as a 'lovely lady', had become deranged from drug use and committed suicide in Paris. It seemed that all the fun and games were almost at a standstill.

One day, I was sitting hidden in an armchair near Idina at Muthaiga. I was alone with a book held in my hands. She was only a few yards away at the bar, regaling two handsome young officers with the story of her trip to Rwanda with one of her best friends, Rosita Forbes. They had gone there to look at the gorillas. Deep in the jungle, they had come across the society millionairess Edwina Mountbatten, married to Lord Louis. She travelled with her sister-in-law Lady Milford Haven and her long-time lover, Bunny Phillips. It all sounded so exotic to meet up with such illustrious personages in the middle of the jungle. I wondered if Joss and I might go on such trips after the war and mingle with famous people. Certainly, Joss was an aristocrat of the highest order. I sat there in a pleasant glowing dream of previously unimagined glamorous excitement, mixing with the great and the good, or more likely the well-connected and the scandalous. I was sure that once Joss and I were married, we would be accepted by these glamorous people who were presently turning their noses up at me. I was seen as a bottle-blonde floozy who had married a peevish old man for his money and was now publicly humiliating him with a very indiscreet liaison with a man who seemed to have slept with every attractive woman in Kenya.

A few days later, a second anonymous note arrived in Jock's pigeonhole at the club:

Do you know your wife and Lord E. have been staying alone at the Carberrys' house at Nyeri together? What are you going to do about it?

Jock didn't show me the note at the time, but it came out at the trial.

On 12th January, Jock and I had a dinner party at our house. We had invited Gerald Portman, Dicky Pembroke, Miss Lampson, Joss, and Gwladys. Unfortunately, the evening was ruined by Gwladys and Gerald having a bitter, violent and utterly pointless argument about whether England or the Colonies had made a greater contribution to the war effort. After dinner, the group moved into another room for dancing, and I went upstairs with Gwladys. We had a heart-to-heart over my situation with Joss and how I felt about him. It turned out that Joss had also had a private chat with Gwladys about his feelings for me. She told the court later that he had said he was very fond of me and determined to marry me. Gwladys advised us both to make a clean breast of it. I told her that I didn't want to hurt Jock, but she insisted that I was young with my whole life ahead of me, and this was a real chance for Joss to find happiness.

Gwladys then took matters into her own hands and talked to Jock. She really was a very managing woman who wanted to control the action around her. Some people thought she was in love with Joss, but he told me she had set her sights elsewhere. Even though Jock had now suffered this unpleasant revelation, he invited Joss to stay the night. Joss wasn't concerned about how old Jock was feeling. It was part of his famous contempt for the feelings of cuckolded husbands. He was not called the 'restless groin' for nothing.

Then, we headed up the coast to June's house at Malindi. At this time, Hugh Dickinson took one of the few photos of Joss and me standing beside an army car on the Kilifi ferry. I don't know how often I have gazed at this photo and thought wistfully how things might have worked out differently if Joss had not been murdered.

Malindi was eighty miles north of Mombasa. The humidity was extremely high at ninety per cent. June's house was large and airy. All the windows were flung open, so air could flow through the rooms. Most people opted to sleep on the veranda in wooden framed beds with mattresses filled with kapok, lying on bases of plaited coconut webbing. Each bed had its own mosquito net.

June showed Joss and me to a more private bedroom. She proudly explained that they had just put in ceilings so that we would be shielded from the *makuti* roof, which housed snakes and geckos. June was pressing gin and *madafu* upon us. This was a drink with generous measures of gin and the juice of an unripe coconut which is opened before the flesh is formed.

"Let's go down to the beach," suggested Joss. "The surf here is huge, and it will be cool and refreshing."

I put on one of the half dozen swimming suits I had brought. I chose an azure blue with thin sunshine-yellow stripes. We held hands and ran into the surf. I had never swum in such a sea; the crashing waves and white foam were exhilarating. Joss held onto me, and we felt ourselves tossed in the waves together.

That evening we sat in the garden beneath huge silvery baobab trees with glistening boles that looked like the columns of vanished temples. We luxuriated in the heavy scent of frangipane and the warm spiced sea air. The palms and casuarinas shivered in the briny air. The sun, orange and round like an incandescent lozenge, moved lower in the sky and disappeared quickly. I hadn't gotten used to the sudden sunsets of an equatorial land.

The boy brought us tea in the morning with goat milk and plain biscuits.

"You know they can't keep cows here because of the tsetse fly," explained Joss.

June bounced into our bedroom with a bushbaby in her arms. She loved animals, and this little creature had unblinking, huge, round, velvety eyes and little human hands.

"It's so cute," I cooed. "Like a mischievous elf."

"It's related to lemurs and monkeys," said Joss.

"Its voice is like a lost child," said June. "It's just the most darling thing. I feed him on fruit, and the *toto* catches insects for him."

I wondered why June had never had children, but perhaps animals were easier to love.

Joss and I had a chance over these days to discuss the future. He advised me to invoke the pact so that I might have the £5,000 a year for the next seven years. I didn't think this was entirely fair, and I was reluctant. I suppose I should have seen the situation more clearly at this point. I was bedazzled with the idea of becoming the Countess of Erroll.

I have to admit that I didn't consider Joss's financial position properly. I assumed that with an aristocratic title came wealth. Moreover, I was very new to Kenya. I didn't have an in-depth knowledge of the inhabitants of this strange land. Joss was the 22nd Earl of Erroll, the Hereditary Lord High Constable of Scotland, and Baron Kilmarnock. His position in the British aristocracy was high, taking precedence over dukes and every other hereditary honour, second to blood Royals. The title of Lord High Constable had been conferred on Joss's ancestors by King Robert the Bruce in 1314 for aiding the defeat of the English at

Bannockburn. It was an office that combined the functions of Secretary of State and Commander in Chief.

I guess I assumed that he had private wealth that matched his titles. He had inherited Oserian from Mary. I had not realised that he couldn't afford to live in it.

Joss later told me, "But everyone knows I have no money!" However, everyone didn't include me. I was the common little bottle-blonde *arriviste*, struggling way out of my depth.

On 18th January, the situation was coming to a head. Four of us sat down to lunch at Muthaiga, Joss, June, Jock and me. Joss went back to his office, June was chatting to a friend, and I told Jock I wanted to talk to him after lunch. Near the veranda's edge was a large bush of red hibiscus flowers. I focused on the sharp yellow stamens, avoiding having to look into his narrow old man face. Finally, I blurted out, "I'm in love with Joss." I dragged my eyes away from the flowers to see his reaction. He was visibly upset. He had been drinking heavily in the last week or two, and his complexion was an ugly florid hue. He was losing his customary disdainful composure. I realised that beneath his thin veneer of sneering arrogance was a weak man who desperately wanted to be respected and liked.

To give him his due, he wasn't going to give in immediately. He tried his best, suggesting that perhaps I was seeing too much of Joss. I looked at him in sheer disbelief. He seemed to be living in an alternative universe of sublime denial. He reasoned that some time apart would help me determine if the affair was serious. He was trying to buy time. Spending three months with him in Ceylon was unthinkable. I told him the truth. I was indisputably in love with Joss. But Jock persisted along his own line. He wanted me to go away with him to Ceylon, to give our marriage another try. He promised he would stick to the pact if I still wanted to leave him when we got back.

I didn't want to be dragged along on a tide of drama, with the hounds of doubt and anxiety snapping at my heels. I refused to consider Jock's suggestion. I knew that Joss and I were deeply in love and that it was undoubtedly no passing fancy on my part. I was anxious to be off on my new life. It was but a hop, skip and a jump away. I was fearful that the prize would be wrenched away from me at the last moment. I remembered my old grandmother warning me that you never really know what manner of man you have until you try and get away from him. I was relishing the thought of never having to see Jock again. There was something rather grand about the prospect of burning my boats.

After our uncomfortable discussion, Jock went inside and rang Joss at his office, saying they had to talk. He said, "Don't you think you should see me, Joss?"

They were to confront each other at Joss's house. According to Waiweru, Joss's personal servant and the gardener cutting the grass, Jock got there before Joss and rudely marched straight into the house and demanded that Waiweru serve him a whisky and soda.

The servants observed the conversation between the two men and reported that Joss was quiet, passively listening to Jock's diatribe that was delivered in a loud voice, banging the chair with his fist. Jock even suggested that Joss should go away for a while and leave Nairobi. Joss pointed out that he was doing important work, and there was a war on.

Jock's final plea was that I should stay in the house at Karen until he went to Ceylon, even to stay there for three months until he got back. He didn't want me to move in with Joss in that time.

All this drama was pushing me to the edge of hysteria as I thought about the conversation that was going on between the two men. Shaking with nerves, I couldn't bear the suspense and dragging June with me, we walked in on their conversation. Jock took June to one side and began to piteously present his case, claiming that he was being made to feel like an intruder. She told me later that he was hinting that he might commit suicide. This was typical of such a weak-minded self-pitying old man. Joss and I went into the house, and he made us cocktails which we swallowed like medicine to ward against the evils of the moaning, jealous Jock. Then three of us went to Muthaiga, and Jock morosely returned to the house with his driver. Joss, June and I stayed on at the Club. Once Jock was out of the way, our mood lifted. I felt light and fizzy, hoping that we might start to celebrate now that it was over. We sat down to dinner with a crowd of others laughing and joking. Jock stayed alone at the Karen house.

That night Joss presented me with the Mary's pearls, three divine strings he hung around my neck, doing up the clasp and breathing in my ear in a way that sent delicious shivers down my spine. It was such a symbolic gesture, as if he were claiming me, and I felt their pearly warmth rubbing on my skin. June and I returned to the house that night and bunked in together because I told her I was scared of the creaking old house. We caught Jock staring at us through a crack in the doorway.

June was not frightened of Jock, which is not surprising since her own husband was a known sadist. She taunted him, saying, "It reminds me of that play based on Agatha Christie's murder story, *Love from a Stranger*. You know the triangular *roman*." Then she tittered and hissed between her teeth. I was humiliated for Jock, but undeterred, he entered the room and began questioning me about the pearls.

Then he came up with the most ridiculous thing. To make his point, he began to quibble about the ownership of some pearls, for which I had paid half in England. Jock had been supposed to pay the other half but, at this point, hadn't. So, he asked me if I wanted to pay them out and keep them, or did I want him to pay the whole lot and take them over himself.

That morning I went downstairs with Joss's pearls still around my neck. That afternoon we had guests. Derek Erskine's family rode eight miles across the country on horseback to our place. There was also Gwladys, June and Joss. We had fun splashing in the pool. Jock got drunk and angry in equal parts. Then, he stumped upstairs and stood at a window looking down at us, frowning and glowering. I didn't like him brooding over us. When June left to drive back to Seremai in Nyeri, I said I would go with her. I was frightened to stay alone with Jock.

Inevitably, we went to Muthaiga rather than to Nyeri. We stayed at Joss's house. Later on, it was claimed that June and I were lesbian lovers. That really wasn't the case. I was not and never have been sexually attracted to women. I was always amazed at how other people's imaginations ran riot when it came to my love life. I believe they were projecting their own fantasies and desires onto me.

While I was away that day, Jock reported the theft of two revolvers from the mantelpiece. Later, the whole trial seemed to centre around the disappearance of those revolvers.

Each day leading up to the murder is etched in my memory. On the 21st, Jock and I went to see lawyers about the divorce. Our trip to Ceylon had been cancelled, but now Jock re-booked his own passage. He also wrote to his chum, Jack Soames, about the robbery and that he was giving up on our marriage.

Apparently, a third anonymous letter was placed in his rack at Muthaiga:

There's no fool like an old fool. What are you going to do about it?

There has been so much written about the events that led up to the shooting. There have been endless interpretations of Jock's behaviour. What was going on in his mind? What were his intentions? Was he plotting? Was he genuinely trying to be decent about our separation?

By the morning of the 23rd, he was talking to Lizzie Lezzard, who described him as difficult. He was still dithering about what he was going to do. We had lunch at Muthaiga with June and Joss, which was rather peculiar, as if we were playing our parts in the last act of a play.

Chapter Six – Murder Most Foul

That night we were to go out for the infamous 'celebration dinner' where Jock toasted Joss and my happiness. At the time, I just thought I wanted to move on from this torturous last dance with this old man I had never loved and had not even wanted to marry. However, Joss was now becoming sceptical about Jock's benevolent attitude, and Lizzie Lezard said, 'it smellt bad'.

The dinner party was arranged during lunch, so Jock returned to the house at Karen for his dinner jacket and a dress for me. He had intended to return to Muthaiga by five pm as he had arranged a golf croquet game with Mrs Barkas, but it was raining, so they went inside and played backgammon instead. Nevertheless, he kept up his pleasant patter, telling her he was looking forward to dancing that night.

Joss, wearing his military uniform, drove June and me up to the Club sometime between six and seven that night. Jock met us in the driveway and took Joss aside. They sat in the back of the Buick together. Jock asked how I was. Joss replied that I had been upset, but he had soothed me, and now I was fine.

After that, Jock played bridge with Mrs Barkas until eight o'clock, when the drinking began. During the meal, Jock got to his feet and made the most mawkish of toasts and wished us happiness and may our union be blessed with an heir. At the time, I was squirming with embarrassment. It was as if he were my father and giving me away to a potential suitor, or I was a parcel being handed around. Finally, he raised his glass and said, "To Diana and Joss."

That night, Gwladys slid up to me and hissed in my ear that Phyllis Filmer was about to return to Kenya. Joss's most recent lover had been away settling her boys into school in South Africa. Although June had told me that Pheely Weely, as they called Phyllis, was surprisingly unglamorous and not Joss's usual type, I did feel that she might constitute a threat. No one I ever spoke to understood Joss's attraction to this woman. They put it down to Joss's renowned impulsivity and unpredictability. That was probably how they explained away his infatuation with me. Perhaps Phyllis was 'good in the feathers' despite her unprepossessing appearance. I didn't respond to Gwladys's spiteful comment but knew that I would have to be on the alert.

After the dinner, Jock made his infamous request to Joss to drive me the sixteen miles back to the house at Karen by three am. I had only spent about five nights at the house since the beginning of January. Joss was willing to pander to Jock's request. He reasoned that June would be with me to safeguard me from any attack from Jock.

Jock took me out on the veranda after the meal and assured me I had nothing to worry about. He was going to Ceylon. I assumed he was trying to save face and avoid the pitying social jeers. However, he did ask me to stay at the house in Karen until he returned from Ceylon and then stay with him until he sailed back to England. Later, when it came out that Jock's reason for leaving England was due to whispers of fraud and his impecunious state, I did wonder. But, in this respect, he was true to his word and did return to England, even if it were only to loiter around the grounds of Dodington Park and then commit suicide.

This ghastly dinner party ended two hours later. Joss and I escaped and went dancing at the Claremont Road House. Jock and June stayed behind and were drinking liqueur brandy. Later in the evening, Jock's good mood reportedly gave way to peevishness, and June said that he was saying things like, 'I'm not going to give her £5,000 per year, and she can bloody well go and live with Joss'

There were other witnesses to June and Jock at Muthaiga. Mrs Barkas, Captain Llewellyn, Jocko Heath and Gerald Portman were having supper and invited June and Jock to join them. Jock just kept complaining and said he wanted to go home. Jock's chauffeur drove them back to Karen at about two o'clock in the morning.

Wilks, my ladies' maid, was still up and saw June help a very drunk Jock up the stairs, and they went to their respective rooms. June asked Wilks for some quinine as she was suffering from a bout of malaria. Wilks took it to June's room, and they talked for a while. June later claimed that after ten minutes, Jock came to her room and asked if she were alright.

Joss and I returned to the house at Karen at about quarter to three. Jock had given careful instructions that I was to enter by the French doors, but the key wouldn't turn, so I went in the front door. I had no idea why he had stipulated that I enter through the French doors, but questions were asked about this later. Although we had been putting up a good show of high spirits that evening, I had become increasingly niggled by the idea that Joss's latest fling before me, Phyllis, was returning to Kenya. I had also become aware of Jock's rocky financial situation and the fact that even if he wanted to comply with the pact, he might not be able to pay. I had also overheard some gossip about Joss's impecunious state and speculation that his involvement with me would come to nothing as he was notorious for always choosing rich wives.

On the drive back to the house at Karen, I was fractious, and Joss and I had our first exchange that was not heavily laced with sexual innuendo and dreamy infatuation. I had suddenly woken up to the fact that Joss was not quite the most eligible man in Kenya. He had left Idina after he had gone through most of her money, and although he still owned Oserian, when Mary had died, most of her fortune had been spent.

I was overwrought from the stress of sitting through that dinner that had made me cringe. Jock had acted as if he were my father, benevolently handing me over to a young suitor. He had no right to act like that, and it seemed to belittle the enormity of the love and attraction that Joss and I had for each other.

Later in court, June gave evidence that I went to her room, and we talked. This was June's ploy to help me. She had assured me that she would give evidence to defend me. She knew the truth. Joss and I had argued, and then he had gone to leave. I was so enraged that I couldn't just let him go. I got back in the car with him. I couldn't bear to be cut off in the middle of an argument. I wanted him to tell me the truth. It had also become evident that even if I divorced Jock, I would not be able to remarry for three years. Someone else had hissed in my ear that Joss was famous for saying that after three years, all passion between a couple was spent. I reasoned that our red-hot passion was so intense that it might take less than three years to fizzle out.

Joss was rather tight-lipped. I knew that he disliked hysterical women. It turned him off, but I couldn't help myself. My blood was up. Jock was a pathetic old man, but he was a protector of sorts. Also, if I was divorced, I might be deported in the same way that Alice de Janzé had been when she returned to Kenya after divorcing her first husband.

We rocketed down the road in the rented Buick. Joss always drove as if the devil were on his tail. He loved speed. I could hear my voice had gone up at least an octave. I was behaving like a hysterical woman, and I couldn't stop myself. I felt as if the world was crumbling beneath my feet. I had taken a step away from those dizzying moments of infatuation and feeling 'in love'.

As we approached an intersection, my rant was cut short. The rank smell of sweat assailed me. A dark figure loomed behind us. He had been hiding in the back seat. I turned my head to look over my shoulder and could see the shiny metal surface of a gun reflected in the moonlight. There was a flash and the acrid smell of a gunshot. Percussion waves boomed in my right ear. My mouth opened, and I screamed. Joss reacted instinctively, flinging up his left hand as if to ward off the arm that was brandishing a gun between us. I began to scrabble in my purse where I had a small handgun. I had been carrying an ornate pistol in my purse ever since we had arrived. I liked the idea of an exotic accessory.

Terror was shooting through my veins, making my limbs heavy and my fingers clumsy.

It all happened so quickly, and it has replayed in my mind for so many years that I can now no longer remember more than a series of flashing images. There was a second shot, and Joss slumped forward. I was still screaming, my mouth wide-open. The car slid off the road to the right and rocketed across the ground. It slid part way down into a murram pit. As it came to a halt, I knew I had to escape. There was the smell of hot blood, and Joss wasn't moving.

I opened the passenger door and threw myself out of the car, rolling clear across the ground, rough dirt grating on my bare skin. I had not changed out of my evening dress before I left. My senses were hyperalert, and I was conscious that the assailant was moving in the car. For a moment, I lay very still, clutching my handbag, the gun now in my hand. Looking back, I am surprised at my quick reactions. I thought I would have frozen in fear and remained immobile. I lay for a minute, trying to catch my breath. I saw the back door swing open. I knew that the assassin would be out in a minute, undoubtedly aiming for me. I had to run. I clambered to my feet and began to sprint away across the road and into the dark. My heart was pounding so loudly that it sounded like a drum. I felt a searing pain across my back, stumbled and rolled into a dip. I looked over the rim of the hole and saw the black figure heading my way.

With a shaky hand, I lifted my gun and aimed and fired in his direction. I knew that I had no chance of hitting him, but he did stop. He was motionless in the dark. I aimed again, holding the gun with both hands and this time I fired with more accuracy. I seemed to have frightened him. He turned and sprang away.

Car headlights were coming from the direction of Nairobi. In the dark, I couldn't see the colour or model. The shooter ran towards it, the sheen of his black skin, his loping stride and a metal gun in his hand silhouetted. I began to shake. Horrible understanding was seeping into the edges of my mind. My adrenalin levels were high, and although I had felt the pain in my back, at this point it had not overwhelmed me.

The black figure climbed into the car that did a three-point turn and headed back toward Nairobi. I kneeled on the ground and vomited acid bile. Then, getting to my feet, I stumbled back to the car looming over the pit. The engine had been turned off, but the lights were shining towards the ground. Joss's body had fallen headfirst into the well of the front passenger seat, curled over like a Muslim praying. I reached in and felt for his neck to see if he had a pulse. My finger came back sticky with hot blood. He was dead. I could not save him. Rage and grief mingled with the pain shooting across my back. Dimly, I realised that I must also have been shot.

I stood there for a moment in the dark, wondering what to do. I could not save Joss. I was worried that the killer and his henchmen might come back for me. Inconsequentially, I noticed that it was a starry night. I headed back down the road towards Karen. As I moved, I could feel the pain throbbing through my back. I imagined that I might be leaving a trail of blood. It didn't occur to me that the smell of blood was likely to attract lions which were known to stalk that area. Panting with pain, I pushed on. I had to get back to the safety of the house. A vision of the side of Joss's head with the sound of the gun and the dark hole in his skin was searing through my mind, fractured images flashing across my inner eye.

Eventually, I stumbled up the drive. I got in through the front door, dragged myself up the stairs, and then fell into June's room. She was lying on the bed, snoring lightly. I got to her bed and fell over her.

"Help me," I gasped.

"Diana!" exclaimed June, coming out of her sleeping stupor.

"I've been shot," I gasped and collapsed across the bed.

Although June would best be described as an airhead, she reacted calmly. She turned on the light and examined my body to find the source of the blood. I think she was used to violent altercations and injuries, having been married to JC for many years. I can't remember much. June forced me to swallow some pills. She always carried a great deal of medication, and soon the calming, dulling effect of morphine took over.

She must have dressed my wound and gone around cleaning up any blood trails I left in the hallway and up the stairs. She undressed me and hid my evening dress which she later disposed of. I crawled into her bed, and she got in beside me after she had finished cleaning up.

"Was it Jock? Did he shoot you? Where is he?" she asked.

"No, Joss is dead. Someone shot him in the head. It wasn't Jock," I replied.

June was up the next morning and answered the telephone when it rang at nine o'clock. It was Gerald Portman calling from his office. He told her that Joss had had a motor accident and had died of a broken neck. June told Jock, who was pottering around near the telephone, trying to listen in to the conversation, clearing his throat and sniffling. A few minutes later, two inspectors, Swayne and Fentum, arrived and began asking questions, writing down Jock's answers.

June came up to tell me what was happening. I was dumb with shock and pain. I rushed to the bedroom window and stared down at the policemen when they left the house. I was thankful they hadn't come up to talk to me. I couldn't stop crying, my eyes aching and swollen. I knew that Joss was forever gone from my life. He was the first person I had ever loved with true passion. Being beside him at the moment of his violent death, being shot myself, the malevolence of his murder, and the fear that I might also be assassinated was sending me insane, dizzy with grief and fear.

I told June about my love letters to Joss, which I had hidden in a notecase in a box of tissues at his cottage. She drove me over there and stayed in the car while I retrieved them. I collected some other things, nothing of material importance, photos, Joss's pyjamas and his forage cap. Later, the police took away all the rest of Joss's correspondence, but they didn't get the letters. While I was there, Lizzie Lezard turned up. I was talking to myself, 'He would have wanted me to have this.' I also took Joss's three dogs with me to care for them.

Although I knew that Joss was dead in the tiny rational part of my mind, I begged Jock to go and see if the body was my beloved. I might have thought it was all a nightmare if it wasn't for the searing pain across my back. I was crazed with grief and fear. Joss's face was playing around the edge of my sight. I could hear his voice in the wind soughing through the tree's boughs outside the window. I was sure that Jock was taking a bizarre delight in this drama. It made me cringe that he should have behaved in such a macabre way. Dimly, I was beginning to put together the pieces, and I was sure that it had been Jock who had hired a black assassin. Everything that he did smacked of thinly veiled delight at the murder of the man who was stealing 'his blonde'.

When Jock arrived at the mortuary, he found Alice de Trafford and Gwladys Delamere had got there before him. Nairobi had always been famous for gossip, and the news of Joss's death had flashed around at the speed of light. Alice had placed a piece of tree on the body, which by anyone's standards, was bizarre. Gwladys had asked for Joss's identity disc. Jock wasn't permitted to enter but asked the policeman to take my handkerchief and place it on Joss's breast. Apparently, he said to Inspector Swayne, 'My wife was very much in love with Lord Erroll.'

What Jock did next confirmed my worst suspicions of him being involved in arranging the murder. He had cancelled our tickets to Ceylon. Now he re-booked them. When he got back, we sat down to lunch. Juanita, June's fifteen-year-old step-daughter, and her notorious governess, Isabel Rutt, had arrived, and we all ate together.

That afternoon Jock made a big show of lighting a bonfire. I cannot imagine what he thought unless he wanted to stage a performance to eliminate incriminating evidence. Perhaps it was a type of ritual celebration of the death of his rival. Juanita reported that she saw a pair of gym shoes on the bonfire. But, of course, in Africa, one never burns second-hand clothes, especially not shoes. Anything like that was given to the servants. Perhaps Jock was not particularly *au fait* with the custom of white people in Africa. Who knows? I don't really care. But much was made of this during the trial.

The day after the murder, my maid, Wilks, left my employ. She went to stay with a neighbour, Mrs Napier. She never gave evidence at the trial. Later they said that I had been attempting to force her to give a false version of the events of that night. She knew that Joss and I had been arguing. That was all she could have possibly known that would contradict our official story. I was sure she didn't know that I had left the house with him, nor had she heard me return.

I couldn't bear to be at the house at Karen. June suggested that she drive us back to Nyeri. She wanted to get me away in case the police tried to question me, and it became apparent that I had been injured. We left Jock behind. He was the last person we wanted around. Anyway, he was on the telephone with Gwladys describing all the events of the previous twenty-four hours as if he were practising his story and wanted to get his alibi straight. I hated listening to him go over events, boasting, and undoubtedly congratulating himself on the result of the shooting. Even if he hadn't organised the murder, he was certainly revelling in his rival's death.

I didn't attend Joss's funeral, but Jock did. He was late and made an ostentatious show of throwing a letter I had written to Joss into the grave. Everything with Jock was such a pathetic performance. He talked to Gwladys at Muthaiga afterwards. He was all over the place, abusing me, saying he wanted Vera back, going through his story that I wanted to go to Ceylon with him. It was all too much for me. I was raw with pain that throbbed in my back. The violence of the shooting reverberated and flashed across my mind whenever I shut my eyes. I was not ready to accept the timelessness of death. If only it had been Jock who had died, not Joss. My lover had been standing on the cusp of a new stage of his life where he would take up the mantle of leadership. At that point, I didn't know that this was why his life had been cut short.

I could have told the police what had happened. I'm not sure why I didn't. Instinctively, I kept my mouth shut as if in some way I was guilty of something. Perhaps, it was the fact of my love for Joss that had led to his murder. Once I had kept quiet, and June had lied, it was impossible to confess that I had been on the scene. I was afraid that the police would charge me.

I know that many people blamed me for what had happened. Particularly galling was Idina's utterly unforgiving attitude. Obviously, Joss was the victim, having been shot and killed, but I was also a victim, and no one cared about me. No kind visitors offered comfort with murmurings of sympathy and soft looks. I did not receive the normal condolences due to someone whose loved one had died in sudden and terrible circumstances.

June, Juanita, the governess and I went to Seremai. The police travelled there to get our statements. We made sure to stick to the story that we had rehearsed. June was an accomplished liar, and she certainly didn't like the idea of being dragged publicly into a trial.

Two days later, Jock drove to Nyeri to join us, and that was when he had his famous conversation with Juanita, a sad little teenager who suffered from the abuse of her father and his cohort, the governess, Rutt. When none of us was around, Juanita took Jock down to the stables to see her pony. Many years later, it came out that Jock had confessed to Juanita that he had somehow been 'responsible' for Joss's death. He may well have told an impressionable child this information. How he could possibly have thought that a vulnerable girl should be burdened with this sort of unsolicited confidence, I can't imagine. Whether or not he was involved in the murder, he should never have foisted such a burden upon Juanita. She was a fifteen-year-old child who had been physically and emotionally abused by her father and governess for many years. Eventually, after a particularly brutal beating, she went to the police and asked them to describe her wounds in the police book. Finally, she managed to escape and went to live with her uncle, aunt and cousins – relatives of her mother, who had died many years ago. Whether Jock really did confess to her or had imagined it is a moot point. It certainly didn't come out at the trial.

Jock was peevish and didn't like the idea that I had not been at June's house when he had arrived. I hadn't eaten for four days. Of course, I had been dosed up with morphine which takes away one's appetite. I was utterly convinced that it had been Jock who had organised the murder. His strange behaviour in the days since the murder confirmed my suspicions. He closely questioned June about what she had said about his mood the evening before the murder.

June was getting nervous and wanted to go down to South Africa, where her husband was staying. Jock made a great point of telling her that she was a principal witness, and she would have to testify at the trial. He seemed aware that he was now the prime suspect and thought that June would supply him with an alibi. He had to make yet another statement to the police about the stolen revolvers, the marriage pact, and even lighting his wretched bonfire. Then Poppy, the chief investigator, headed to Jack Soames' house at Bugaret to pick up spent bullets and cartridge cases.

I was never questioned about the murder beyond taking my statement. I was hysterical for days. This was reasonable considering my experience and the fact that I had been shot and injured. June gave me some hefty painkillers, and this helped to some extent. Even if I had not been on the scene and shot, I'm sure I would have still been in no fit state to answer searching questions.

I was cut off from Joss in the first early stages of our love affair. We had had our first argument, and instead of resolution and renewed love-making, and protestations of love that would transcend all obstacles, there was nothing. Blank, staring emptiness, and the sound of my voice was accusing and cruel as I asked him how we were going to survive financially.

Assistant Inspector Poppy was a good investigator, dispassionate and thorough. That's what made it so strange that no physical evidence had been collected from the scene. No fingerprints were ever taken. It was obvious that Poppy thought us a rackety crowd compared to the early settlers who had become heroes in their own lifetimes, such as Lord Delamere, Sir Francis Scott and Ewart Grogan. He disapproved of June, who was rather silly, calling him Popski. She was known for her loose morals. However, despite his disapproval, he treated me kindly.

After the murder, I went on safari for eight days with Jock, Hugh Dickinson and others. We went to southern Maasailand, along the Mara River. I was afraid of Jock and thought he might be planning to kill me. His savage changes of mood, the malevolence in his nasty eyes, his pursed mouth, and his general twitchiness made him very unpleasant to be around. Dear Hughsie Daisy suggested the idea of the safari, and I felt safer out in the open in company, accompanied by John Hunter, who was a big white hunter.

It was strange to hear the smooth snick of cartridges pushed into place and then bullets whining away against the wind. It was different from the blast right next to my ear as that second bullet had found its mark in dear Joss's head.

Amazingly, I even managed to shoot my first and only lion. This animal is the most sought after of all the hunting trophies. I had seen his round, tawny face staring at me through the long, golden grass about seventy yards away. John, our white hunter, was at my shoulder, his gun raised in case I missed. He let me judge the distance, and I squeezed the trigger.

At night we sat around a crackling pungent-scented campfire. I edged close to John Hunter and drank, hoping that the ghosts, the *shetani,* and spirit orbs, not to mention the wild animals roaming in the bush around us, would be held at bay by the bright, warm flames.

On 10th March, after we returned from safari – seven weeks after the murder - Poppy came to the house at Karen and quietly arrested Jock. They took him to Nairobi Police Station, and he was locked up. His lawyer was Lazarus Kaplan.

I was alone in the house afterwards, my nerves jangling. I had thought that perhaps I would also be arrested. That, somehow, they knew I had been on the shooting scene. Nevertheless, I was still not thinking straight. Then an Indian man appeared in the doorway. He was impeccably polite and self-effacing and introduced himself as Sidney Fazan, the Provincial Commissioner at Nyanza, stationed at Kisumu. I had no idea what he could want with me, but I invited him in.

"I hope you will forgive this intrusion," he began. "We must speak with much confidentiality."

"Of course," I replied, "Would you like tea?"

He declined my offer graciously. He spoke in a roundabout way as if he did not want to get straight to the point. He said he blamed himself for what had happened and wrung his hands. Eventually, he explained why he had come.

"Joss came to see me about one month ago. Joss was afraid. He knew that he was in danger. I told him that he should enlist and remove himself from the danger. Alas, perhaps I should have urged him to take greater precautions."

I stared at him. Joss had known he was in danger, and it was probably nothing to do with me or Jock, in spite of all the dark suspicions that had been cast upon us.

"Who was trying to harm him?" I asked, breathless with trepidation.

"He did not know, but it was something to do with the natives," replied Fazan, his kind brown face looking doleful.

Joss had known he was in danger, but he didn't know from whom. This did not shed any light. In fact, the mystery was deepening.

"He must have had some idea," I snapped, my nerves twisting.

"Did you know he was shot at, some weeks before?" asked Fazan, hesitantly.

"Yes, the bulletproof glass in the car," I replied. When he told me, I had not really given it much thought. He had mentioned it so carelessly that I had assumed it was unimportant.

"He thought it was because of what he had said, you know, in the meetings, he told everyone that he was a fascist. Now with the war, a fascist is seen as a very bad thing," said Fazan, his kind brown eyes staring at me with sympathy.

Of course, I had no idea what Joss had said in the meetings. I knew that he spent an inordinate amount of time attending meetings of this and that, speaking all over the country, promoting his views, many times in opposition to the ideas of others. But, to shoot anyone with a different perspective was pretty extreme, even in the depths of Africa.

"Are you going to talk to Assistant Inspector Poppy?" I asked fearfully. Somehow, I felt that such a conversation would not bode well. I was afraid that Popski would interpret the information as further damning proof that the murder was related to Jock and me.

"I do not think Joss would want me to. It was very confidential," replied Fazan. "I do not really know anything, but I felt I should tell you."

"Do you think I am in danger?" I asked.

"No, it was a political matter, and you are not involved in the politics of this country," replied Fazan.

I thanked him for visiting me and agreed that the matter should remain confidential. After he left, I sat staring into space, thinking deeply. Politics – could it be related to fascism? Although I knew that Joss had long since distanced himself from the British Union of Fascists, perhaps it had not been enough. I shrugged my shoulders. There seemed nothing that I could do. The house felt strangely empty now that Jock had gone to prison. I would have to go down and see if he needed me to take him some things. Or perhaps they would let him go after charging him.

One of the worst atrocities of the murder went more or less unremarked: no one had told Joss's daughter. Her name was Diana, but she was always called Dinan. She found out by seeing the headlines in the newspaper at the local shop where she was living with Idina's sister, Lady Spicer, in Wiltshire. She was only fourteen years old. Later, it was said that she suffered from the horrible things that people were saying about her father. His reputation as a womaniser was cited as the reason for his murder. None of the good things he had achieved in his life were reported. The press seemed to want to blacken his character completely, and the story of how Mary's previous husband had attacked him with a bullwhip was widely circulated.

Jock had to stay in prison for three months until the trial. June and I visited him two or three times a week. Alice de Trafford, surprisingly, visited him nearly every day. I wondered if it wasn't part of her rather macabre interest in the occult, a man soon to be tried and who would be hanged if found guilty. Perhaps she was fascinated with the thought of a person teetering on the edge of the abyss, ready to descend into the underworld.

Jock managed to comport himself with dignity in prison. He had his food brought in for him, and he had quite a number of visitors. As well as meals, he had a supply of chocolates and cigars. As a white man, he had special privileges and paid one of the other prisoners to clean his cell. Every evening one of the warders would take him outside for half an hour's walking. I suspected that beneath his urbane manner, he was quite desperate, but he kept up appearances.

I found out later that Hugh had smuggled in a syringe of morphine in a chocolate box, so if the verdict went against Jock, he would commit suicide rather than hang.

Three weeks before the trial, we still had not managed to hire a defence counsel. There were none in Kenya, and none could travel from England in wartime. Although I still suspected Jock of hiring an assassin, I decided that I should be seen to do the right thing as a wife, if not faithful, at least not uncaring. I flew to Johannesburg and managed to hire

Harry Morris, K.C. He was well-known for his flashy and belligerent style of court behaviour. We had to pay him £5,000, and it turned out that this was probably the last of Jock's money. He had never had the money for the pact. I couldn't help but wonder whether Joss would have married me without the £35,000 from Jock. He had said we 'would manage somehow', but now we would never know if he would have stuck by his word or given me up for a woman with more money. If he had become Kenya's leader, there would presumably have been a decent salary.

Jock had been corresponding with an old friend in England, Marie Woodhouse. The letters have been examined over the years, looking for clues to Jock's state of mind. He was afraid and had written, "In a strange country, God knows what will happen."

He was also reported to have asked Poppy, "Do Europeans hang in this country?"

If Jock had known the truth of that night, that I had been a first-hand witness to the murder, he would certainly have put me in, to save his own miserable skin.

Chapter Seven - The Trial

The court case began on 26th May and ended on 1st July. The Chief Justice, Sir Joseph Sheridan, presided. The Attorney-General, Walter Harragin KC, prosecuted for the Crown. The Court House had a domed glass ceiling. The spectator gallery was overflowing. The different sets of people in Kenya were there in force. The class division between the Happy Valley and Muthaiga crowd and the po-faced, sanctimonious bunch who oozed disapproval of the louche behaviour of Joss's group was much in evidence. I was the focus of everyone's attention, hated by both the Muthaiga crowd and the others. They thought my actions had put the whole country to shame, especially during wartime.

Joss's ear in a small glass jar was handed around. At that point, I couldn't stand it and rushed out. It took some time, but I managed to pull myself together and returned to my seat in the gallery. At the trial, I learned the usefulness of self-possession to mask vulnerability. I had always worked hard on how I looked. Now, I focused painstakingly on every detail of my appearance. I felt the only control I had over my life was the outer cloak of clothing and makeup, and my expression and demeanour. I could not bear for the world to see my pain. Joss had always maintained an immaculate and perfectly groomed appearance. Somehow, doing the same, made me feel closer to him.

Sitting in court, I was conscious that I was the object of Idina, Phyllis and Alice's venomous hatred. I could feel their eyes boring into my back. I knew they had each loved Joss, as I had and wished they would accept me and share their grief with me. I feared that that was never to be.

I must have got something right as the *East African Standard* began to report on my outfits, for example, "Lady Broughton was again in court wearing a dress of polka-dotted cocoa brown crêpe, with a small white collar and short sleeves. Her tiny brown felt sailor hat was tied at the back with wings of veiling." This was one of the outfits I had bought in South Africa when I went down to hire the defence counsel.

They said that I was hard, and I'm sure that all their efforts went into cracking my veneer. There is nothing to give one strength more than other people trying to make you show your suffering. I remained stalwart, putting on my makeup and elegant clothes and carrying it off. In private, I crumbled, but in public, I kept up appearances. Survival depended on never letting other people see your distress. It was the rules of the jungle that prevailed at boarding school.

The newspapers covered the trial extensively, not just in Kenya but also in England. One aspect of such interest was that two aristocrats were at the centre of the story, the 11th Baronet of Doddington standing trial for murdering the 22nd Earl of Erroll, Chief of the Hays and Lord High Constable.

The Crown's case was weak. It depended entirely upon the evidence of their two ballistic experts that the shots fired at Joss came from one of the revolvers that had been reported stolen from the house at Karen.

Jock often boasted of his performance when he took the stand. It was his primary line of conversation afterwards. It was strange. He was in his element. He had always craved attention and seemed to enjoy being on stage. June also performed well, especially considering that she was lying through her teeth. She had been rehearsing in front of a mirror.

After deliberating for three hours and thirty-seven minutes, the jury acquitted Jock.

Immediately after the trial, we went to Muthaiga. It has been called a 'celebratory dinner' which was not the truth as far as I was concerned. I think it was that dining at Muthaiga was what we did. We had been eating meals there regularly since we arrived in Kenya.

Shortly afterwards, Jock and I boarded the *SS Union Star* and sailed for Ceylon. This was the much-discussed journey that Jock had constantly used to try and separate Joss and myself. It didn't really matter to me where I was at that point. In other circumstances, I might have enjoyed such a trip travelling through the tropical woodlands, admiring the rice paddies straddling mountains, gazing at elephants who stood by the roadside, next to ancient temples engulfed by sweet-scented foliage. One could see large wild mongooses and monkeys running around the coconut plantations. At night flying foxes leapt among the branches.

A giant flat-topped rock called 'Fortress in the Sky' rose over 400 feet above the surrounding countryside. In the fifth century, the King Kashyapa had built an impregnable fortress city on this rock, covering three acres with gardens and exquisite buildings

Ceylon had not escaped the war, and there were men in uniform buzzing around. I saw some of them looking at me with my bottle-blonde hair, and it reminded me of when we had first arrived in Nairobi and gone to Muthaiga, and I had enjoyed being the centre of attention. If only we could travel back in time. Anything to change what had happened. Why had we agreed to go back to the house at Karen that night? If we had only gone to Joss's cottage and spent the night, nothing might have happened. Or, perhaps, the killing would have been arranged at some other time. It hadn't been a random shooting. It had been a planned assassination.

Despair clouded my entire being like ink from an octopus. I felt fettered, choked with grief.

Jock spent a great deal of time writing letters to people in England, particularly Marie Woodhouse, who was known as a 'hard woman to hounds'. I never really worked out whether they were just friends or whether they had had a sexual connection in the past. He was trying to ensure that he would be accepted in society when returning to England.

The malicious stories about me ever since the murder stung and I retreated into my shell. The comments were usually along the lines that I was 'hard' and my light-blue eyes were 'like ice'. I cannot help the colour of my eyes, and I find it strange that such a physical characteristic should be used as the defining feature of my personality. It wouldn't have mattered if I had poured myself into all sorts of philanthropic works. Instead, they would accuse me of satiating my sexual lusts. I can only think that people projected their own fantasies onto me. Some years later, I discovered that Barbie Lutyens, the woman who had stolen the heart of Euan Wallace, Idina's first husband, had very strange light-blue, icy eyes, which might have explained the depth of hatred that I had felt from Idina.

On 27th September 1941, Alice killed herself when we were in Ceylon. During and after the trial, she had been involved with Dickie Pembroke, who had made a determined attempt at courting me before he had settled for Alice. He was a handsome man and very wealthy, but he lacked a title, and I had decided I wasn't interested. He came a poor second to Joss. I supposed that Alice was not thrilled that she had been his second choice.

Perhaps Alice, then over forty years old, not in the first flush of youth, chronically ill and drinking too much, was not as attractive to men as she had been. It was well known that Dickie's priority had been to get back into his regiment, the 3rd Battalion Coldstream Guards. He had been put on temporary leave because of an affair with a fellow officer's wife. Nevertheless, he had treated Alice well.

A few weeks after the end of the trial Dickie was to rejoin his regiment. Alice travelled with him as far as Kampala in Uganda. She returned to Kenya and was due to have a hysterectomy. Then, bizarrely, she shot her beloved dog, Minnie, before she went into hospital. It seemed a very morbid action, especially for a woman famed for her love of her animals. She even wrote to Dickie about the fact that life need not go on, 'In Joss's case someone decided that, in Minnie's case I did, and the length of our own lives lies entirely within our own hands – unless someone else gets to us first!'

I remembered reading somewhere that one of Alice's friends had said she 'smelled of death'. She had chronic bronchitis, and it seemed she had been obsessed with the Great Beyond.

Alice buried the dog herself in a flower bed. In the following days, she went to visit Joss's grave. A few days later, she asked her staff not to disturb her. She decorated her bedroom with armfuls of flowers, wrote five letters, wrapped bandages around her chest, and took a huge dose of barbiturate. It began to take effect, and she shot herself in the chest.

I had heard that Alice had suffered from severe bouts of depression all her life. It was assumed that these had worsened, Dickie going off to war, and her hysterectomy added up to push her over the edge. In terms of my goals in life, to have a title and wealth, I wondered whether these things weren't guaranteed to make one happy. Alice had been extremely wealthy, and her first husband had been a Count. She had had beauty and two daughters, even though she lived halfway around the world from them and didn't seem to want to be near them. Happiness was a strange commodity. At that time, I was extremely unhappy, but Alice's suicide made me think about what I wanted in life. I became determined that I wouldn't let myself go downhill as she had. I was still young and somehow had to rise from the wreckage of Joss's death.

Eventually, we got back to Kenya. Jock was behaving erratically, and he decided that he would make me happy by renting Oserian from Erroll's estate. This house had been a huge incentive for Joss to marry Mary Ramsay-Hill, and now it was being used again as a chip in a marriage deal. I believe an abode is the sum of its occupants, past and present. One interesting idiosyncratic fact was that Cyril Ramsay-Hill had a penchant for pornography and had an extensive collection safely locked away as it was illegal in Kenya. Mary likely used this fact to negotiate the deeds of the house in the divorce settlement.

Oserian meant 'place of peace' in Maasai, built in 1925, commissioned by Cyril Ramsay-Hill. The estate included 5,000 acres on the shores of the freshwater Lake Naivasha. It had been modelled on Cyril's grandmother's house in Seville. It featured graceful arches and a fountain murmuring in a tiled courtyard, marble columns, domes, frescoes painted by Italians and Indian teak floors. In the large central room with an impressive cupola, delightful small alcoves scooped like ice cream out of the walls. Mary had added furnishings to the house, including a random collection of white polar bear rugs scattered around the drawing-room with a massive inglenook fireplace.

Immediately after Joss's death, it had been rented by Prince Paul and Princess Olga of Yugoslavia. They had lived there with their children under house arrest. Now, Jock and I moved in. We were not under house arrest but were social exiles. It was just as well we were out of Nairobi. It was clear that we were not welcome at the Muthaiga Club or any other meeting places of the white ex-pats. It might have seemed strange that we went to Joss's former home. I think Jock was taunting me, but I was happy to be anywhere that was associated with Joss, clinging to my last shreds of love for him.

Jock was drinking vast amounts of alcohol and injured his back soon after we moved into Oserian. How he actually did this is lost in the mists of time and untruths. One version was that he fell from a railway embankment. Another was that he was drunk at Percy Wheelock's place and fell down the stairs. Jock had always been like that, more worried about what other people thought than actuality. Lying was second nature to him.

In August, Jock wrote to a Nairobi lawyer, Humphrey Slade, citing my supposed affairs with other men. There was an Italian, an officer on the boat to Cape Town, another man who was on honeymoon and then, of course, my affair with Joss. Jock also suggested that I should be prosecuted for staging a fake robbery of the pearls in the south of France. He tried to blackmail me with this and sent me a letter trying to force me to return to England with him. I had shown the letter to Poppy, who said I shouldn't worry about it. At that point, I just never wanted to see Jock again. I was going to have to organise a divorce, but in the meantime, the more miles between us, the better.

Chapter Eight – The Gilbert Years

Jock sailed away, and I was left alone at Oserian. Morbidly, I relived every moment I had spent with Joss. In the dark empty hours of the very early morning, I remembered what he had told me, that Bram Stoker had said that the Errolls were subject to dark rituals and blood sacrifice. Perhaps blood sacrifice was more likely to happen on this Dark Continent. I shivered despite the heaped bedclothes and got up to swallow some whiskey to try and dull the aching pain. Sharp, bitter twists of the knife were stabbing at me. Finally, a handsome, charming man had been dangled before me and snatched away after a vicious blood crime. Perhaps, Joss hadn't been entirely decent, but he was undoubtedly a prize for any woman.

Gilbert Colvile was my neighbour. He was a strange, reclusive man who was kind to me. Unfortunately, not many people were kind to me after the trial. Although it had been Jock on trial, it seemed that I was the one who was judged guilty. Before he left, Jock hated the burgeoning friendship between Gilbert and me. His farewell action was to write a poisonous little note to Gilbert, "*You've got the bitch. Now buy her a kennel.*"

Gilbert did not comment, but I could see his compassion for me in his eyes when he showed me the note. He was a tough, strong, silent man. He had never been a part of the chattering classes in Nairobi, but had been a good and decent friend to Joss. Although Gilbert was scorned for having 'gone native', he came from an old, noble family. His father had been Sir Henry Colvile, a member of the Grenadier Guards, a distinguished soldier with many medals. He was Assistant Commissioner in the Foreign Office in Uganda from 1893 until 1895. He died ingloriously, not in battle, but knocked down by a bicycle in Bagshot in Surrey.

Gilbert was an only child. His mother was Zelie Isabelle de Preville, descended from the French aristocracy. In his youth, Gilbert had blown off several of his own toes while shooting rabbits, preventing him from taking up his commission. When Sir Henry died, Gilbert and his mother came to East Africa for a shooting expedition. They decided to stay. They sold the estate in Lullington, near Burton-on-Trent and bought a farm called *Ndabibi,* in Naivasha. Gilbert's mother opened a hotel at Gilgil.

Gilbert was a great admirer of the Maasi, and he could speak their language fluently. They say that Lord Delamere was also a great admirer of the Maasi, but his attitude differed from Gilbert's. Whereas Hugh Delamere indulged them, forgave their misdeeds, and listened to their opinions, giving the herdsmen a free umbrella every year to shade them from the sun, Gilbert certainly didn't give them free umbrellas. Nevertheless, the Maasi accepted Gilbert and called him *Nyasore*, a lean man. He didn't patronise them but adopted their austere lifestyle. He lived in a shack with his dogs. It was furnished with imperfectly cured animal skins. Over time, he added more rooms and panelled one with lion skins. He had a Maasai herdsman clutching a spear in the front seat of his car when he drove into town. When he was out in the bush, he wore clothing made from the skins of antelopes to protect himself from thorns. I believe that the idea that indifference to the opinions of others is a mark of true aristocracy. Certainly, Gilbert was no adherent to middle-class British mediocrity.

I asked him about the Maasi, and he drove me for hours across the plains until we arrived at a *manyatta*, a collection of little huts where the Maasi live.

"They have very important customs, you know," explained Gilbert. "A young warrior called a *moran*, who has raided and stolen enough cattle to qualify, will give his chosen one a gift of honey. That is the first step. After that, she will drink the honey, mixed with milk, with her sisters, those with whom she has been circumcised."

"It puts it all in perspective," I shuddered delicately at the thought of circumcision. Gilbert chose to ignore my distaste for such a barbarous custom.

"More honey is given, and honey has been fermented, making it alcoholic for the elders to drink. Eventually, the young man is told that his offer has been accepted. The skins of a calf and sheep are used to make the wedding garments. The groom brings more gifts from animals on the wedding day. The bride is covered in honey, and ritual ornaments, such as coils of copper wound around her limbs."

I smiled at him. He seemed to be bringing up the subject of marriage, perhaps thinking that we might be wed. It was a tentative and roundabout way of suggesting it to me.

"I don't find those elongated ear lobes at all attractive," I commented. Gilbert shrugged.

When we drove back to Oserian he presented me with a pair of diamond earrings. They were large stones, exquisitely cut. I took off my small gold studs and tried them on. I turned my head this way and that, gazing at myself in the ornate, gilt-edged mirror that hung on the wall of the drawing-room.

"Thank you, dear Gilbert," I said, kissing him lightly on the cheek.

He flushed a deep red and soon took his leave, returning to his house next door.

Gilbert was passionate about fires and loved setting a stretch of dry grass or a bush-clogged gully alight. He enjoyed watching the roaring flames. I think he saw something ancient and unchangeable in the mutable shape of the fire, forever moving but always constant. He lived off a diet of meat and bananas, and if ever he drank, it was sherry. He had adenoids which might have explained why he spoke so little.

Despite his eccentricities, perhaps because of them, he built up the country's largest cattle herd. He began importing pedigree bulls but realised that such big-boned animals needed a high protein diet. This was not provided by the veld grass and made the cattle more susceptible to disease. So, he replaced his pedigree bulls with native Boran cattle, hardy Zebu animals from the north. This decision meant that he owned one of the country's best and biggest cattle herds.

The beauty of the surroundings of Lake Naivasha had a beneficial effect on me. The birds began to cry in the early morning when the sky was pale pink. Dew evaporated into the warmth of the day, and the silvery tones of the landscape melted into gold. The calm, soothing lap of the lake wavelets against the green sward that stretched down the hill from the house was healing. The screaming agony of shock at the murderous violence gradually dimmed, and I became numb. Then slowly, slowly, I began to come back to life. I sniffed the cool air and felt fresh life flowing through my veins. Finally, I began to edge away from the torturous labyrinth of my unanswerable questions. Was it that I did not deserve love? Had my life pursuing wealth and brittle social success forever disqualified me from true love? Was my marriage to Jock so despicable that I deserved to be trapped forever?

Gilbert pandered to my longing to talk about Joss and would tell me about the days at Naivasha when Joss and Mary had lived here. Joss had begun a yacht race called the Erroll Cup, and Mary would present the handsomely engraved trophy that had been brought back from London. Gilbert had won the cup in the first race in 1933 with his boat, the *Quest*.

I would walk around the beautiful gardens and gaze at the fish-eagles and pelicans perched on tree stumps along the shore. Standing beneath a fig tree considered sacred to the Kikuyu, I remembered my magical moments with Joss. Sometimes emotion would overcome me, and I would crumple, tears streaming down my face. The weight of sorrow crushing me, leaving me choking on the pain, merciless grief overwhelming me. Gilbert found me like this one morning, lying in a heap on the grass near the boundary between Oserian and his property. He insisted that I go with him to check on one of his farms.

We drove many miles, and I remember staring stonily out the windows. When we arrived, we were greeted by the Somalis, clad in their traditional long chequered *kikoi* robes and tomato-red or gentian-blue turbans wound around their heads. They were a very proud race, with clever, bony faces and dark velvet eyes.

"The Somalis have been moving south for more than six hundred years," Gilbert told me, "One of their legendary ancestors was meant to be Mohamed the Prophet, and they first set foot on African soil from the shores of the Red Sea. They're as tough as their ponies, cunning and full of intrigue. They're split into small clans and constantly at war with each other. I guess it keeps them on their toes."

"How devout are they?" I asked curiously.

"Well, there is no purdah, and their women don't wear the bui-bui with only slits for their eyes like the Muslim women at the coast," replied Gilbert.

We mounted Somali ponies and rode out onto the plains. Somehow, seeing the world through a horse's ears lifts one's spirits. The plains spread out around us, my spirit rose, and I looked out onto a vast world. A place of opportunities for me. I was alive I had nearly died that night but had survived. I had to believe that Fate had a plan for me. I knew beyond doubt that my future lay in Africa. I associated

England, the dark and gloomy world of war, with Jock having gone back there, where he belonged.

That night Gilbert talked again. This time he spoke about the long history of Kenya. It helped to put the drama of the current world war and colonial rule into context.

"You know that there were human skulls found from probably millions of years ago. As early as 2,000 years BC, there were waves of migration. The Turkana came from Ethiopia, Kikuyu, Akamba and Meru from West Africa, Maasai, Luo and Samburu from southern Sudan. Trading along the coast has been going on for thousands of years. There has been Arabic, Persian, Indian and Chinese merchants trading ivory, skins, spices and gold."

"It puts it all in perspective," I said. "The British and their Empire is only a tiny part of a long string of conquerors."

"Movement of groups and individuals around the world is not a new thing. It could be somewhere better to live, commercial opportunities, religious quests, better climate. The musical chairs don't stop because one government wants to hedge people into particular areas from which they're not allowed to move. It is organic, the desire of humans to move somewhere else, to find something better."

"There is something about Kenya that is special. It's not just the beauty and wild spaces. There's something in the air beside the spitefulness of the little English who bring their closed minds to this land," I replied sadly.

A few weeks later, Gilbert took me on an expedition riding up the slopes of Mt Kenya. It was believed that when He was present God lived at the summit. We followed a track that elephants had made. There were tall cedar trees that in later years were to be plundered. Then, tall bamboos rose above us like a feathery arch filtering the lambent green light. Higher we climbed and came out on a strange type of moorland, giant groundsel like cabbages on stalks and furry scaled lobelias. This shifting scenery and trail that led us upwards raised my spirits. I was sure that Joss would have enjoyed such a journey and imagined that I was living an adventurous life in his stead, carrying his spirit with me.

In December 1942, the news that Jock had committed suicide at the Adelphi Hotel in Liverpool was announced in the Kenyan press. He had taken an overdose of Medinol. I am not ashamed to say that I was intensely relieved. It would save the ghastliness of a divorce. I believed the world would be better without that self-pitying, pathetic old mess. I still blamed him for hiring an assassin to kill Jock. Gilbert was watching to see how I received the news.

"I'm fine," I said to my stalwart companion brightly. "It's the best ending we could hope for."

I knew what he thought - that now we could marry.

More details about what happened to Jock when he returned to England filtered through. The only people to meet him off the ship had been two detectives who Poppy had tipped off to investigate him for fraud. There was no hard evidence, and he made his way back to Doddington Park in Cheshire. He stayed at the butler's house on the far side of the park, not approaching the big house, which had been turned into a wartime school. There was a record of him telephoning a solicitor, Eustace Bowles of Market Drayton, on the 24th of November. He told him that he had been thrown from a horse, which was the source of his injuries. He went to see Vera, who was living with her mother and tried to persuade her to return to him, but she refused. He saw a lot of Marie Woodhouse, to whom he had been writing letters since he had been arrested. Apparently, he even boasted to her that he had carried out the murder. But, of course, I knew this wasn't true. It was typical of Jock to lie to project an image. In spite of his suicide, his casket was placed in the family vault at Broughton parish church.

In January 1943, Gilbert married me, hardly one month after the death of Jock. I knew that this would create a fresh wave of gossip. No one would have expected it. We must have appeared as a very odd couple to the outside world. I was as outgoing and social as he was introverted. I didn't care. It would be fair to say it was a *mariage de convenance.*

I had almost told Gilbert about being shot by Joss's assassin on our wedding night. He had seen the scar on my back. I told him it had been a shooting accident, and I didn't want to talk about it. He didn't press me. He was wonderful like that. He never demanded personal confidences, respectful of privacy.

Being married to Gilbert gave me a huge measure of security, not just financial but also emotionally. There was cruel gossip but my outer shell thickened to the point of being impregnable against the inevitable barbs and slurs. Gilbert seemed entirely unconscious of malicious gossip. He lived in his own world, peopled with Maasi, cattle and visions of the wide-open plains. Somehow his love for me had grown within this circle of existence, and I joined him riding amongst the cattle beneath the blue-blue arc of the African sky. He moved into Oserian with me, and we decorated the marble veranda with a huge lion skin, which Gilbert had speared.

I had resolved that I would be a perfect wife for him. Not being in love helped. I respected him and was very thankful that he had overcome his dislike of even talking to women to offer me marriage. I found it easy to be bright, cheerful, and supportive. I never snapped or whinged. I coaxed him into making small changes in our lifestyle, but I didn't insist that he turn into a luxury-loving, cosmopolitan person.

In the same year that we married, Gwladys Delamere had a stroke and died aged only forty-five. Phyllis Filmer was still living with Idina up at Clouds. They got on well, acting like land girls producing gallons of milk with Idina's famous dairy herd.

Although Gilbert was impervious to social pressures, he was extremely acute regarding business decisions. He was said to be the richest man in Africa. He paid £12,000 for Oserian, which was put in my name. It was my wedding present. It was ironic that Jock had foreseen this outcome when he had sent the poisonous little note saying that Gilbert should buy me a kennel. Gilbert was generous with the big things like that but penny-pinching when it came to smaller expenses. He already had a house at Muthaiga, opposite the golf course. He also purchased a house in Kilifi for me. It was a two-bedroom white-painted bungalow with a long, arched veranda facing the ocean and an orchard of mango trees behind it. He knew how much it meant to me as once Joss and I had rented it during that brief time when we were together.

Gilbert made other gestures to celebrate our wedding. He agreed to move into Oserian and made some effort to improve his style of dress. He made over some of his lands to me and suggested I buy a string of racehorses. It was through racing that I was able to re-enter the margins of the social world of Kenya. I loved horse riding, and I thought that perhaps I might become friends with Beryl Markham if and when she ever returned to Africa. I began to go out dancing again, and Gilbert sweetly agreed that as he didn't dance and I would need a partner, I should be accompanied by Jack Hilton. We used to go to the 400 Club in Nairobi. I enjoyed the shades of my former life in London. I adored Gilbert and would never speak against him, I called him 'Pooey'. People used to say that before he married me, he had a homosexual obsession with the Maasai warriors. But then, as I have learned, Kenyans will gossip and make up the wildest and weirdest stories about everyone.

We imported a pack of Atherstone hounds and hunted lion and buck. We took pinches of snuff which were kept in pouches around our necks. I called it *Eau de Boma*. It cleared the mind and the head and made you see the track more clearly.

My personal life had been so eventful that the war faded into the background. By the beginning of 1942, the Ethiopian campaign, which had begun at the same time as Joss's death, was over. Seventy thousand Italian prisoners of war had been brought to Kenya and had to be housed and fed. They were put to work building a good tarmac road from Nairobi to Naivasha. The road followed the original route over the Escarpment and down into the Rift Valley. This was going to be a boon for those of us who lived at Naivasha.

Italian POWs were working on the railway, and the rest were interned in large camps at Gilgil, Nanyuki or Eldoret. The focus of the fighting had shifted. Japan had entered the war and advanced through south-east Asia. It looked like they might move across the Indian Ocean and invade Africa on its eastern shore. African soldiers were quickly trained in jungle fighting and shipped to India, Ceylon and Burma. Black and white Kenyans fought side by side in Madagascar against the Vichy French.

Ironically, Kenya's economy was hugely benefited through the war. Mombasa was an important port. Kenya was a staging post between Britain and the Far East. There was a silver lining in this cloud. Kenyan farmers had an insatiable local market for anything they could produce and, for the first time, made good money from selling their produce. Many Kenyans who had enlisted in the army were given early release to go back to their farms and work on food production. The army took to shooting wildlife, particularly in the northern Laikipia plains, which thinned down the population of wild animals.

Although Gilbert and I were relatively socially isolated, we did hear the story of how Idina had been reunited with her long-lost son, Gee. She had not seen him since she had left his father Euan when he was a toddler. Gee had been posted to Kenya, found her at Muthaiga and danced with her all evening. He was summoned and castigated by his superior the next day. "She's old enough to be your mother," he was told. "She *is* my mother," he had replied. Idina had a few months to get to know her son, meeting up with him whenever he had leave, and he also went to Clouds to visit her. Then he died, as did his father and his brother in the same short time period.

In July 1943 the newspapers were full of the breaking news of the brutal murder of Sir Harry Oakes, in Nassau in the Bahamas. He was one of the richest men in the world, a rough diamond who had found gold in Canada. It was a bizarre and gruesome murder and his son-in-law, a man called Fred de Marigny was accused of the crime. The fact that the Duke of Windsor, the brother of the King, was the Governor of the Bahamas had inflamed the situation. Curiously, he had personally taken charge of the investigation and obtained the services of two corrupt Miami detectives to gather the evidence. Local policemen were not allowed near the investigation.

The newspapers were drawing parallels with the murder of Joss. Beyond the fact that Nassau was a British colony, as was Kenya, the court cases took place during wartime, and Joss was known as a philanderer and de Marigny was represented as a playboy, there were no meaningful likenesses in the two cases. In the matter of Sir Harry Oakes murder the prosecution's case hung upon two fingerprints and there was a great deal of time taken up during the hearing about the veracity of these prints. Similarly, during Jock's trial there had been much made of the ballistic evidence. The only other tenuous link was the Duke of Windsor. Joss had been on good terms with the Duke and it had been suggested that his knowledge of the Duke's affiliation with the Nazis had been the reason for his assassination. This was not the case in the murder of Sir Harry Oakes. The Duke had taken an active part in attempting to orchestrate the conviction of an innocent man, de Marigny. Eventually, it came out that he had done this to deflect attention from his own nefarious crimes of money laundering which involved the real murderer, Christie, the murder victim, Sir Harry, and also a maverick figure, Wenner-Gren, who was the organiser of the illegal movement of currency around the world.

Soon after the conclusion of the case when de Marigny was found not guilty, another assassination took place in Cairo. The victim was Lord Moyne. Immediately, the rumours began flying around Kenya that somehow there was a connection with the shooting of Lord Erroll. Both men had been the lovers of Jock's wives. Apparently, Jock had written to Lord Moyne from prison asking for help in his trial but had been summarily dismissed and told that he should let the legal process take its course. The chattering classes relished the fact that Jock's first wife's lover, Lord Moyne, had been assassinated, and Jock's second wife's lover, Joss, had been executed. Jock was pronounced the kiss of death.

The story was that Lord Moyne, who had been serving as the British Minister of State in the Middle East, had been assassinated by the Zionist paramilitary group, Lehi. They were Fighters for the Freedom of Israel, also known as the Stern Gang. They wished to eliminate the British authorities in Palestine and allow unrestricted immigration of Jews and the establishment of a Jewish state. What was truly bizarre to my untutored political mind was that they thought that Nazi Germany was less of a threat to the Jews than the British. Apparently, there was a lot of illegal Jewish immigration to Palestine during the war.

Chapter Nine – The Post-War Years

Finally, the war ended, and the black Africans who had fought overseas returned to Kenya, having seen and experienced many things. They did not fancy going back to their reserves, growing and harvesting two small crops a year, and herding their goats. Nor did they desire to be lowly-paid farm workers on white men's farms. They gravitated towards the bright lights of Nairobi, to the beerhalls and the brothels, the bazaars and other men who had shared their wartime experiences. There were not many jobs, only the Asians had employment, and there was a seething atmosphere of anger and disillusionment.

In 1946 Mosley published *The Alternative,* which proposed that Africa should be used as a garden estate for the more civilised European races. A special type of white man should be bred to carry out this project. Viewed through the lens of post-colonialism, this was the epitome of white supremacy. I wondered what Joss would have thought of such a theory. Would he have been influenced by Mosley and run with such an idea? I feared that he might. He had wanted Kenya to flourish in its own right, not merely to send provisions to England, but he had undoubtedly viewed the blacks as a race that was lower down the social scale.

Mosley's book was not well-received in England. He and Diana had been released from Holloway Prison in 1943, where they had been incarcerated for more than three years. The public feeling against them was intense. A hostile crowd stood outside the prison gates, erecting a scaffold. Communist protestors gathered with banners and painted slogans, and the press cackled like jackals. It reminded me of my experience at the trial when I had been the focus of public outrage.

Eight days after their release, there was a huge protest in Trafalgar Square with banners and slogans and a gibbet with a dangling effigy of Mosley. Two Labour MPs petitioned the House of Commons demanding the immediate return of the Mosleys to prison. Ninety delegates representing 20,000 factory workers marched to London with another petition. It seemed that every person in England resented the release of the Mosleys and was sure that they would return to their subversive ways. The wave of emotion that not only swept through England but beyond was astounding, and the hatred of the mob was terrifying.

In 1947, British rule ended in India, and many Indian Army officers and administrators decided to settle in Kenya rather than return to England. Indian craftspeople and workers, who had depended upon the now-defunct British Raj, followed them to Kenya rather than suffer in the messy and dangerous Partition exercise where the Hindis settled in India, and the Muslims went to two separate areas named Pakistan.

The events of my personal life continued to occupy me. I thought I would never have suffered such grief as I experienced after Joss's death. But then I lost my baby daughter, Sarah Colvile, who died after just ten days of precarious life. This broke my heart. I thought I was going mad, drifting away into a nether world of despair. I had so much wanted a baby, a tiny bundle of love which had grown within my body. She died in September 1947, and her epitaph read "*So Little and So Short a Time*".

I lay in the hospital bed for some days. Gradually, my body got over the upheaval of childbirth and the nurses bustled around me, thumping pillows and making bolstering comments designed to lift me out of my post-partum misery. They were sympathetic but brisk and bracing. They made me get up and walk to the shower. They encouraged me to dress. I put on one of my maternity dresses and saw that already my body was losing its pregnancy shape. My waist shrunk, and I could wear anything in my extensive wardrobe again. I took strength from my smart clothes. They provided a shield against the world that had often turned its cold gaze upon me.

Gilbert arrived at the hospital to take me home, finding me dressed, my hair brushed, and powder on my cheeks. He smiled at me uncertainly. I appreciated then that he shared my feelings and was there for me. He didn't say much, but his sympathy and compassion enveloped me.

The depths of agony were not an unfamiliar place. Again, I began to question my worth as a human being. Was I so unworthy that God would not give me even one child that would love me? Had I sinned so terribly that I deserved only to be cast down into a pit of despair? I shut my eyes, and all I could see was my baby's sad, malformed face. I could not escape this vision and knew I had to bear it until I could go beyond the terrible pain. So, we went home, and Gilbert and I tried again. I got pregnant several times but always miscarried.

One evening I was sitting on the veranda, wrapped in a soft lambswool blanket, gazing broodily down to the lake, which shimmered in the moonlight. The full moon in Africa is fuller than anywhere else in the world. The shapes of the trees glimmered silver casting black shadows. Slipping out from the darkness, a black woman came up the stairs. The kerosene lamp illuminated her profile. Her bare feet slapped on the wooden surface of the veranda as she approached me. She was tall, with a proud bearing, dressed in traditional clothing, a bright bandanna wrapped around her head but no ochre paint on her body. Her musky smell assailed my nostrils. I stared at her, surprised at her confidence to approach me without invitation or permission.

"There is a curse," she pronounced in an authoritative voice.

I stared at her in horror.

"A curse," I whispered, feeling as if my skull was being beaten by the shadowy wings of an evil spirit. Usually, I did not hold much store by the myths of the shamans and witch doctors, *mgangas,* moonlight ceremonies, and bad spirits; but there was something about her words that rang with truth.

"You never have children," she stated in a flat voice.

"Why?" I pleaded. A part of me wondered at her use of the English language. Had she been coached in the words before she came to impart her message? Was Jock cursing me from the grave?

She stared at me. Her black eyes blazed with undisguised hatred, then turned and walked away. She had disappeared by the time I was up out of my chair.

Gibbering with fear, I told Gilbert what had happened. He didn't look surprised. Then, I realised that he already knew. The jungle drums had been beating.

"Don't worry about it," he said to me. "It's not true because I have found a child." He was throwing me a lifeline. At first, I turned away from the idea. He waited patiently, and then I saw that it was a solution. Adoption would solve the problem.

"We can go to Uganda. There is a woman there who can arrange it for us. A little girl. She can be yours to love. A white baby. It cannot replace Sarah, but it is something. She will be ours, and we will give her a good life."

A tiny part of me noticed that Gilbert, usually so silent, had become eloquent. Of course, nothing could replace Sarah, but it was a way of climbing out of the pit of despair, a form of ritual purification.

"Let's go to Uganda," I said.

He smiled quietly.

"Are you sure?"

"Yes," I replied. "We must forge on together."

We adopted a gorgeous little girl called Deborah, who I nicknamed Snoo. When we brought her home, I was filled with joy and delight at everything in the universe. Although I later sent her away to school in England, we spent a great deal of time together. She has been one of the best things to happen to me in my life.

One day I was lounging in the garden re-reading Isak Dinesen's book, and Gilbert told me that his mother had been friends with her. I was amazed, which upon reflection, was a silly reaction. Everyone in Kenya knew everyone. Even more so, they knew everything about everyone.

"My mother told me that she had been sure that Denys Finch Hatton would marry her when Bror married Cockie," said Gilbert. "My mother was mistaken. By the time Finch Hatton died, he had taken up with Beryl Markham, although I doubt he would ever have married her. He wasn't the marrying kind."

"No one could believe that you would want to marry me," I said to him teasingly.

He smiled shyly.

"Or that you should want to marry me," he replied.

We understood each other very well, but most of it was unspoken. He was not a conventionally handsome man, rather small and wiry with large ears, which I suppose were good for hearing out in the bush when he was tracking. He had a domed forehead which housed his very acute large brain. Indeed, he was not the demon lover that Joss had been, but I was glad to be with a man so very different to Joss. At least with Gilbert, I knew that he was faithful. Not that many of us set much store in fidelity in those days. We didn't even intellectualise the matter with the rationale that we were following the authenticity of our sexual desires. We just screwed around as the mood took us. Even Jock had been unfaithful to me with my maid, Wilkie. Many years later, I found out that he had asked her to visit him in prison about being called as a defence witness, but in the end, she hadn't turned up at court.

Gilbert and I enjoyed many expeditions, in Kenya but also overseas. I returned to England for the hunting, and we also visited South America and Mexico. Often, we would leave the sheltered shores of Lake Naivasha and travel north to Ol Morani, which meant 'the young warrior'. It was one of Gilbert's ranches in Laikipia. There was no proper house on that property, but we would set up camp in a suitable place. Although there were no dramatic geographical features in that area it had a certain understated charm, the golden dust particles hung suspended in the air, giving it a restful, hazy atmosphere. There were acacia groves, open plains, and bountiful herds of eland, zebra and giraffe. In the distance were the ancient silent mountains and the mysterious gorges.

Some distance away was the Rumuruti Club, a rambling group of cottages built amidst a clump of eucalyptus trees. There was a tennis court and a bar. Usually, Gilbert was not social, but he made an exception in this case. The remoteness of the location and the gathering of such a scattering of far-flung settlers did not lend itself to a cosmopolitan setting which he so disliked. We watched the games of tennis and drank. I would take an evening dress, and Gilbert changed into long trousers and a dinner jacket. There were some descendants of the Cole family there. They were the next generation from Florence Cole, who had been the wife of Lord Delamere. Her two brothers, Berkeley and Galbraith, had lived in Laikipia country.

On one notable occasion we were invited to a *ngoma,* a big festival held by the natives. This was something that Gilbert insisted I must see. The edge of the moon lit the night, and the moving bodies formed shadows on the flat grassy plain.

It was a barbaric black African party where the different tribes clad in their traditional glory came to dance and celebrate. There were the Tharaka in swishing skirts of dried grass, metal rattles encircling their ankles, and intricately painted shields. The Meru in coloured *shukas* and head-dresses. The Turkana women wore bright blue and red bead necklaces, and long gathered skins of serval cats swayed around their lower bodies. The men's heads were covered in decorative oblongs of blue feathers.

There was a wonderful *mélange* of jumping competitions, acrobatic dances, raucous chants, and singing in unison, the voices blending with the night. There was also the rhythmic stomping of feet and deep-throated safari song of the traditional Pokot people, whose women wore long skirts of soft hide greased with goat fat and red ochre. Their necklaces were threaded with bone, leather and wood beads. The men were dressed less garishly in black *shukas*, with long, shiny ostrich feathers attached to their heads.

The dancers stamped in the dust, and the pungent aroma of bush sage and exotic fruit rose and filled the hot, smoky air. I felt my heart thumping in time with their elemental drums and rhythmic notes that rolled from a hundred throats. They swayed through the hazy atmosphere, and I felt Africa's erotic, beating heart. Something that could never be found in the damp, drizzling ambience of the place where I had been born. The dancing was unashamedly sexually suggestive, and I edged closer to Gilbert, feeling the heat of his body by my side. There was a demonic dimension to the long, leaping black shadows flashing across the ground.

Potent fermented maize meal was brewed in large gourds bubbling on flat rocks next to the fires. A bullock on a spit roasted on the fire, and pieces of tough, charred meat were carved from it and passed around. Tactfully, I declined to chew on this delicacy. However, I did sip some of the alcoholic drink and found it more potent than any spirit I had previously imbibed.

We stayed in the camp for several more weeks and rode amongst the herds of cattle. The rains were coming, and we left after the first drenching rainfall. The Highland wind stops in the wet season, and the leaden sky hangs close to the ground. There are clouds of white butterflies that migrate westwards. They are like clouds of snowflakes in an improbable summer storm.

Chapter Ten – Making Sense of It

Our marriage lasted twelve years. Gilbert taught me so many things about Africa and how to live in harmony with this wild landscape. We would kick the dust to test the direction of the wind. We rode about the plains amongst his cattle. The aromatic scent of sage, dung and resin filled our nostrils. I also learned to use Maasai snuff which heightened the senses and helped to keep one going all day. At night we sat around campfires and I learned to distinguish between the roar of a lion, the cough of a leopard the bark of a zebra, and the highly-strung cry of the impala.

It took me a few years to trust Gilbert with my dark secret. It was like a cancer growing in my breast. Then one night, camping out on the plains, staring into the dancing flames of the fire, Gilbert began to talk. I grasped a possible truth that might explain the dark deeds of that terrible night when Joss was shot. The navy-blue velvet African night enveloped us, and bright stars were spangled across the sky. Gilbert was usually a man of few words, but on that night, having drunk two glasses of port, he was almost eloquent. His knowledge of the recent history of Africa was extensive.

"It was after the First World War, that the natives fought for us and came back, and we subjected them to even worse conditions than before the war. Wages were cut by a third, and the natives were forced to wear *kipande* for identification around their necks. This was a little metal case with a piece of paper which recorded the name, tribe and fingerprint, and his current employer was meant to sign him or her on and off. There was meant to be a register of all the people living on every farm. Then came a stream of white settlers, soldiers who came to claim their land flooded in."

"The white men thought that they were bringing a civilising influence," said Gilbert with a wry grimace on his face that was lit by the flames of the campfire. A lion roared in the distance as if commenting on this belief. "The whites broke their promises."

He paused for a moment, then went on.

"This was the beginning of the Kikuyu resistance to the white man's invasion. In 1921 they formed the East African Association. There was also a hut tax. The white man was demanding money from the blacks for the privilege of living in their own huts. They also banned the blacks from growing coffee which was the most lucrative crop. Harry Thuku was the leader of the black movement, and they put him in detention for a trial in 1922. They also killed a lot of Kikuyu who were protesting."

"With increased pastoral activity, growing numbers of stock and restrictions on the nomadic cattle-herding practices of the Maasai, Samburu, Turkana and Pokot and the camel-herding Somali, Oromo and Rendille, soil erosion became a problem. The closure of grazing in the White Highlands exacerbated this. So, the government forced destocking amongst the Kamba and Tugen tribes, resulting in political ferment."

"The problems with squatters' rights had increased with the 1937 regulation that defined squatters as labourers, not tenants and gave power to settler district councils to regulate native stock and labour. However, the number of squatters continued to grow. By the end of the 1930s, more than 150,000 Kikuyu were living and working on European farms, many of whom had lost land rights in the crowded Kikuyu Reserve."

"In 1938 Kenyatta, who was living in the UK, wrote a well-publicised book on the Kikuyu people called *Facing Mount Kenya*. At the time, it was not well-known, but Kenyatta spent two years in Russia studying under an assumed name and funded by the Soviets. Although he flirted with communism, he was not persuaded and was more influenced by the pragmatic British political approach."

"It wasn't just the blacks protesting against the whites that almost passed unnoticed. The most tension was between the Asians and the whites. There was segregation for whites only."

"Now I understand. That's why they called the Aberdares - the White Highlands," I cut in.

"Yes. That's right. There was actually twice as many Asians as whites in Kenya in the 1920s. That was when the Colonial Office came up with that meaningless pronouncement about paramountcy."

"Yes, I remember the jokes at Muthaiga. There was some sexual connotation attached to the word, you know 'mounting'," I said.

"It was called the Devonshire Declaration. It said that in the event of any conflict between blacks and whites the interests of the blacks should always be paramount. But it was essentially meaningless. There was no land allocation for the Asians. The three-tier racial segregation was still firmly in place."

"There was a lot of development. The towns were growing, roads, railways. The whites had to use enforced labour to do the building and farming. The British government tried to play fair with the treatment of the natives, and as you know, there was antagonism between the settlers and the administration. The settlers claimed that the Colonial Office had no idea what was happening on the ground. The settlers were members of the Muthaiga Club, and the administration people were members of the Nairobi Club."

"Yes, I know that Joss felt very strongly about that. That they should be self-governing in Kenya. That is the whites here governing," I said, putting together the pieces with what I already knew and how this fitted into the whole story. "He was also fighting against squatters' rights. I never really understood what that was about."

"Yes, it all comes down to land," said Gilbert. "The squatters were natives who had the right to use some of the land in return for their labour. But the settlers were calling for the cancellation of squatters' rights in case the natives would create a *de facto* right to the land, and they wanted the natives to be forced into labour. You know Joss made a speech about it in the House of Lords when he went over there for the Coronation."

"I didn't know that," I said, wondering how I could have missed the fact that Joss had been speaking in the House of Lords.

"It was widely reported here in Nairobi," said Gilbert. "Everyone was talking about it at the time. It wouldn't have gone down well with the political Kikuyus, the Somali, or

Maasai. I don't think it went down well with the British who truly believed in paramountcy."

I saw his eyes gleaming in the firelight. He was watching me. I sat there thinking carefully. The murderer had been a black man. I had always thought that he was an assassin hired by Jock. Here was an entirely different motive. Nothing to do with what was in the grand scheme of things, a mere infidelity, sexual jealousy and the prospect of a divorce. Everyone in Kenya seemed to have been divorced once or twice. It was no big deal.

Gilbert was silent. I could feel him waiting.

"Do you think that Joss might have been killed for his political beliefs about Kenya?" I asked hesitantly.

"Yes," said Gilbert.

The simple word hung in the air between us. The world as I knew it shifted on its axis. What if it hadn't been Jock at all. That would account for his confident performance in court. That performance that he had boasted about. He knew that he had had nothing to do with the murder, but in a weird way, he had taken pleasure in my suspicions of him. What a despicable man he had been.

"But how does Jomo Kenyatta fit into all this?" I asked. Scrabbling around for something to divert me from this enormous truth that was dawning.

"He was from Kiambu, and in 1929 he was sponsored to go to London to try and make claims on the land. He had been mission-educated, and he had had a job in Nairobi. He had powerful friends in London, including Arthur Creech-Jones, and in the Fabian Colonial Bureau, Also the Pan-African Congress with headquarters in Manchester activated by George Padmore, a West Indian. In the early thirties, many Africans were rendered totally landless. They moved to Nairobi and lost any sense of land belonging to them. The reserves had been made the property of the Crown. This engendered a lot of anger. Another major bone of contention was female circumcision."

I tooted with laughter at this. I knew it was a tribal rite of passage for young women, and I had shuddered delicately and tittered whenever the subject had arisen in social conversation.

"Not exactly a bone," I quipped.

"The missionaries staged a campaign against it like a symbol of the cultural differences between the natives and us," said Gilbert, smiling wryly at my levity.

I needed to think about what he had told me. It was all too much.

The following day, we rode across the plains and onto the plateau so that we looked down on the Rift Valley. In the morning, the plateau table was higher than the sun. At night some stars burned beneath the edge of this geographical wonder. I put aside the intricacies of Kenyan politics and focused on the horses. We had wonderful horses that had been retired from the racetrack and some Somali ponies that were very quick on their feet. One of my favourite mounts was a lovely mare, Goldie, by an extremely well-bred thoroughbred stallion out of a fantastic little Somali mare. Sometimes when you cross bloodlines, you get the worst of both, but it had worked out well in her case. She had the sure-footedness of the tough little Somali ponies but the speed of her thoroughbred ancestors.

Gilbert and I did not discuss the matter of Joss's murder for several months after that campfire conversation. But, the thought that Joss had been killed for his belief that the blacks should never be given back their land had been planted in my mind and it wasn't going away. Joss had never acknowledged that the blacks had a right to the land in the first place.

Then Gilbert showed me a summary of the transcripts of Joss's speeches and, more importantly, the newspaper articles that had reported on this and the coronation. It might have been the information that had sparked off a decision by a group, or perhaps only one politically-minded black African, who had decided to do something about it.

I read the newspaper articles. Then, I ran into Paula Long one day in town. I invited her to come to Oserian, and she accepted. She was an intuitive person, and she had been friends with Joss and the other Happy Valleyites for many years. She had known Mary when she had still been married to Ramsay-Hill. We sat down to tea on the veranda overlooking the lake, and I asked her to tell me about Mary and Joss. I had put together what she said to me with the newspaper accounts.

Mary and Joss had returned to England for the new King, Edward's brother's coronation at Westminster Abbey in May 1937. There was a lot of preparation involved in terms of outfits and protocol. Mary was dressed in a silver and white Norman Hartnell gown to be worn under her crimson mantle.

During that period, Joss made his first speech in the House of Lords. He sat quietly through a speech by Lord Noel-Buxton, who talked about racial relations in the colonies where 'advanced persons lived cheek by jowl with backward peoples,' advocating the principle of trusteeship.

Joss got up and said that anyone who made his home in the colonies was aware that his good examples and teaching of his traditional experience can, to a very large extent, mould native opinion and native life in the right and correct way. He pointed out that a universal policy of race relations could not be usefully implemented across the Empire that would 'meet the needs of all the divergent races, with their divergent habits.' Joss pressed the point that each colony or protectorate should decide their own issues according to the local situation.

Lord Lloyd was one of the members who responded to Joss's speech by stressing that ' . . we ought to be very careful before we encourage any element in the Empire to think that the transference of the protectorates to any other rule but our own, is likely to be feasible in the near future.'

Joss and Mary returned to Kenya, and Joss was elected to the Legislative Council as a member for Kiambu. One of the big things that he spoke up about was the issue of squatters' rights. He stressed that many of the Kikuyu *githaka* rights were fraudulent. He said that large family groups running relatively small areas of land such as 60 or 120 acres meant that the environment was destroyed, that wood and water supplies were depleted, and damage was done to valuable tracts of land.

Paula told me that Joss had seemed to genuinely love Mary and although he'd been having an affair with Phyllis and undoubtedly seeing other women, he had not deserted Mary as time went on. I was tempted to tell Paula what I thought about the murderer, but my experience with the other Happy Valleyites made me cautious. I said nothing.

I told Gilbert what I had found out. He confirmed that he had spoken to some of the Maasai and they had told him that there had been talk of a black assassin. No one was pointing a finger and not a word even about which tribe they might have belonged to. They described it as a 'heavy matter' and would confirm or disconfirm nothing. There was no proof. But Gilbert and I agreed that it most the likely explanation. The reason why such a solution to the mystery had not been proposed was the colonial view that the blacks wouldn't have had it in them to contrive such a plan. The British would only have considered a black African culprit if Joss's head had been hacked off with a *panga* or he had been speared. In view of what happened next, it seemed that the whites, in their arrogance, had severely underestimated the determination of the black Africans to get their lands back.

Chapter Eleven – Meeting Idina

After the war, events were marching on in Kenya. Our country was just a small outpost of the civilised world, but we were somewhat behind many other African nations demanding independence. There were tiny token acts of recognising the blacks' rights but they were not enough to stem the tide of change.

Since discovering that this issue caused my beloved's murder, I paid particular attention to the politics of the time. In 1944 the Governor had appointed the first black African, a British-educated teacher from Kiambu, Eliud Mathu, to the Legislative Council. By 1947, the Labour Government in Britain had decreed that there should be four nominated, not elected, black African Legislative Council representatives. But these tiny concessions were insufficient to hold back what was to come.

By 1946 the Kikuyu was swearing new versions of the traditional oaths to resist anti-squatter rules. That year, Kenyatta returned to Africa to take up a leadership role in the nationalist movement. He took the main oath of unity, the Mbari oath, and the following year, he was chosen as the leader of the political group, KAU. The key issue was the return of 'stolen lands'. The Government began to resist by limiting the number of KAU movements. The administration believed that Black political movements were the cause of the unrest rather than its manifestation.

Around this time, Idina had a nervous breakdown and had to leave Clouds. She went to live by the coast, away from the high altitude. She had a bungalow at Mtapwa Creek, ten miles north of Mombasa, on the banks of a long sea inlet.

I was staying a lot at Kilifi that year. I loved the rarefied atmosphere of the coast, the smell of pungent mangoes, smooth coconut milk, and roasted *korosho* nut. I would take Snoo and her ayah, and we played on the beach, sat around on the deep cool verandas, and I would go fishing. I had taken up deep-sea fishing, which was to become a lifelong passion. Gilbert wasn't keen on the coast. There was nothing for him to do. He didn't mind sailing on Lake Naivasha but had no love of the sea.

I began to brood about the idea of Idina living not so far away from me on the coast. I had heard that she was ailing, and I wished that, somehow, we could make a connection. I had steeled myself against the dislike of so many of the Kenyan socialites, but Idina was different. She was the mother of Joss's daughter, and I knew that he and she had maintained a good relationship after the divorce. For three years after the murder, Phyllis had lived with Idina at Clouds. They had been united in mourning Joss. Idina had always been close friends with Alice, who had also loved

Joss. It was clear that I was excluded from this club and I resented it. I, too, had loved Joss. There had been nothing but jagged and ill-intentioned rays coming my way from this group of women. I had a burning desire to talk to Idina, to tell her that I was not the cause of Joss's death, that it had been about land and how the white people had treated the natives.

I had heard that Idina was the inspiration for one of the characters, the Bolter, in the novel *The Pursuit of Love* by Nancy Mitford. So, I read the book from beginning to end in one fell swoop. It was rather like a novel by Evelyn Waugh, light, frothy, amusing, and very clever. It was based on the Mitford family, which was fascinating as I had been such a fan of Diana Mitford for many years. As I read, I was entranced by the mixture of real people and invention.

The Bolter was the mother of Fanny, who was the narrator. She only made an appearance in the last pages. She was presented as an infamous woman who was known as someone who left each of her succession of husbands and lovers. The depiction of her was unkind. She was a figure of fun who arrived with a Spanish lover who didn't understand one word of English. Based on Lord Redesdale, Uncle Matthew hated foreigners and Juan, the lover, was about to be banished until they found out he could cook. This assignation of Juan to the servant class smacked of the inevitable British superiority complex.

The Bolter did have the final word. She said, 'The lives of women like Linda and me are not so much fun when one begins to grow older.' Fanny had not liked this comparison between Linda, the protagonist and her mother, suggesting that Fabrice had been Linda's great love. The Bolter replies, 'One always thinks that every time.'

This was Idina's life, as Alice had said to me at that party before Joss had been killed. Idina always felt that she had to marry every man she fell in love with.

If one was to identify a Bolter, then I probably fitted the bill better than Idina. After all, Joss, Idina's third husband, had left her for Mary Ramsay-Hill. I had left Vernon Motion, then Jock, and perhaps one day, I would trade in Gilbert for another. Was it so wrong to trade up, to continue to look for 'the one', not to make do with whatever specimen one had married and then found wanting?

I had always been intrigued by Idina. We had even employed Josphat, one of her former employees, in the hedonistic Happy Valley days. Privately, I had discussed with him the things that used to happen. He told me about their white snuff, which I assumed was cocaine. I still hankered after any information related to Joss and his life before I met him.

I certainly didn't envy the way Idina had been presented in this novel. She was a figure of fun, a parody of herself. My desire to meet her strengthened, and I decided that I would go to visit her unannounced. The worst that could happen was that I should be unceremoniously told to leave, escorted to the gate by one of her servants.

I could tell her my beliefs about the murder. Perhaps this might mitigate her dislike of me. I was hardly responsible for Joss's political beliefs, established long before I had come on the scene. I decided not to admit to her that I was there that night. Instead, I would tell her about what Fazan had told me, the bulletproof glass in the car, the fire at Joss's office and the rumours that Gilbert had heard from the Maasai. Indeed, she would see that all this added up to the most persuasive theory of what had happened that night.

I set off one afternoon, planning to arrive at four-thirty, in case she enjoyed the customary afternoon siesta. At that point, she had not yet met Jimmy Bird, nicknamed James the Sixth, as he would have been Idina's sixth husband had they married. It was widely known that Jimmy had a penchant for men and engaged in homosexual affairs. Unlike Gilbert, I enjoyed the company of homosexuals who were very good at discussing clothes and hairstyles. I had had one very bad experience with Fabian Wallace, who had been Joss's friend, and when I had collected Joss's dogs to look after them after his murder, I had also taken Fabian's dog. He had declared I should take it immediately to a friend as he didn't wish me to look after it. But there is a big difference between a friendly association with homosexuals and living and sleeping with one and sharing his affections with other men.

However, at the time that I visited, Idina was uncharacteristically single. I dressed carefully. I didn't want to turn up like a bird of paradise as if I were trying to show off. However, my love of couture and habits of always being immaculately turned out could not be thrown away, perhaps just toned down. They had mocked her in *The Pursuit of Love* for wearing trousers as if they were the latest thing when in fact, during the war years, they had become commonplace. Idina had set the fashion of wearing practical trousers when she had first come to Kenya. Many people were shocked by this behaviour at the time. Undoubtedly, she had been a trendsetter. I chose a simple pencil skirt which came to my knees and a plain white shirt and no jewellery. I hated the way people mocked me for wearing my beloved jewels.

I got the chauffeur to park down the street and approached her house on foot. She was sitting alone on the veranda, wrapped in a blanket, staring into the distance. At first, she didn't seem to register my approach. I was trembling with nerves. Then she looked at me as I stumbled up the front steps and I saw that she recognised me.

She was utterly silent. I was glad she wasn't shrieking like a harridan, telling me to go away, but Idina had always had class, and even a nervous breakdown hadn't taken away her prepossession.

"Good afternoon," I said as I walked towards her, determined not to register shock at her appearance. She had aged since I had first set eyes on her in the early 1940s. She was still bottle-blonde, like me, and her eyes sparkled but were surrounded by a fine net of wrinkles. Her chin had always been her worst point, and it still receded in an unattractive manner. There was an unmistakable pallor to her skin, rouged in such a way that she looked like a clown.

My voice squeaked with nervousness, and I cringed at the sound of it. She continued to stare and didn't rise from her chair. "I hope you don't mind me coming to visit uninvited, but there are some things I wish to tell you," I said, consciously trying to lower my voice, remembering my elocution lessons from all those years ago.

"It's Diana Delves-Broughton," she said in her husky voice as if she were talking to someone else.

"Well, I'm Diana Colvile now," I replied.

"Of course, you married Gilbert. He was a great friend of Joss's," she mused. Her tone was mild, but the implication was that I was so unimportant that my current marital status was of no account.

"Yes, that's right," I replied. "I wanted to talk to you about Joss. About his murder."

She glared at me accusingly, just a flash. Then, she emptied her face of expression and waited. A long moment of silence.

Haltingly, any confidence I mustered was draining away in her presence, I told her my theory about the fire at the Lands Office, someone shooting at Joss's car, and Fazan's account of Joss believing he was in danger. She was looking sceptical, and I was on the verge of blurting out the truth about it being a black and then showing her the scar on my back to prove it, but caution prevailed.

I waited, expecting her to tell me to leave, but she relaxed.

"It wasn't you, and it wasn't Jock," she said slowly.

"That's what I think," I said quietly, my voice hesitant.

"What about the fascism?" she asked.

"But Joss had given all that up, long before I got here," I said. Perhaps she knew more about it than me.

"I remember Tom and Cimmie, witnesses at our wedding," she said, gazing into the distance, slipping back into the past. "He was a very charismatic man. I had an affair with him."

I wasn't surprised. It was exactly the sort of thing that one would expect of Idina, with her reputation.

"What did you think of fascism?" I asked.

"Alice didn't like it at all. She was definitely left of centre when it came to politics. Myself, I had no interest in politics at all. Poor Diana Guinness was caught in that dreadful trap and look how it turned out for her."

Of course, Idina would have known Diana. She was part of that glittering exclusive world, to which. I would never belong, always hovering on the periphery. I wondered if I had been a contemporary of those people, whether Mosley might have chosen to bestow his sexual attentions upon me. There were rumours that Diana had allowed him to take the virginity of her younger sister, Unity.

"You know Joss gave up his career in the foreign office when he married me," she said. "There was no way that a woman twice-divorced would be acceptable in that circle in that time."

"Do you think that he regretted giving up his career?" I asked, trying to puzzle out the course of Joss's life.

"He was keen on the idea of coming to Kenya. He had that very British sense of adventure, but not the early settlers' love of hardship. I had the land, and he called the house Slains, harking back to his ancestral home that had to be sold because the family had lost all their money."

"He told me that he was caught in bed with a maid at Eton," I said, introducing what was often seen as Joss's defining feature, his pursuit of sexual exploits.

"Dear Joss, he was extremely libidinous from an early age. I thought a lot of it was the thrill of deception. If he had gone to Cambridge in the 1930s, he might well have become a spy, but I don't think he had much interest in fighting for universal mankind. He had too much of a sense of deprivation from losing his home. You know I had no idea of his secret relationship with Molly when we were married. We had an open marriage, but he kept his cards close to his chest when it got serious. He was adept at that sort of 'doubleness'. Perhaps he felt more of a man by having secrets."

"Jock said that people hated him and were happy that he had been killed. Do you really think that he was universally reviled?" I asked.

"No, I don't think that was the case. He was very kind, you know, and thoughtful. Especially when he started devoting himself to the betterment of Kenya," she said defensively. "I have to go inside, it is getting cold out here," she continued. I was being dismissed. I saw that she wasn't going to invite me in.

"I didn't like what they wrote about you in *The Pursuit of Love*," I blurted out, sounding as if I were desperately trying to ingratiate myself. She laughed, a tinkling, happy sound.

"Yes, that book. It wasn't very flattering, but the bit at the end, about old age, perhaps that was true. Perhaps I have sucked the best out of life and not left enough to see out my days graciously."

"You're hardly the only woman who has not wanted to settle for a man who isn't right for you, forever. Especially not in Kenya," I added.

"Joss was only an interlude," she said thoughtfully. "A very pleasant interlude, but he was a boy, you see. Although, by the time he died, he had grown into a man."

"I adored him," I stated.

"Yes, he was good at inspiring adoration," she agreed. "But it was more than that. You know the way he cared for Molly, who became Mary, throughout her illness, the kindness he showed, the patience. That wasn't just Joss marrying a woman to fund his lifestyle." She looked about vaguely as if she had suddenly forgotten where she was.

"You should read *The Green Hat.* It was much more flattering. Good-bye."

I was dismissed as lightly and easily as one might wave away a beggar girl in the street. I walked down the stairs, determined not to look back. I heard the door bang as she went inside.

I didn't seek her out again and nor did she try to make contact. I was not accepted into what was left of the Happy Valley circle. I had to be content with having had that one chance to talk to her. In 1955 she died at the age of sixty-two.

The novel *The Pursuit of Love* also gave me much food for thought about the mystery of Diana Mitford's life. It was her family who inspired the Alconleighs, and the character of Uncle Matthew, who was based on Lord Redesdale, fascinated me. I understood for the first time why Diana might have been so drawn to Oswald 'Tom' Mosley. Her father, with his blood-stained entrenching tool had been such a strong influence in that house of women, and she was inevitably drawn to such a man when she grew up. Bryan Guinness had been wonderfully kind and had longed only for her return after she had so cruelly spurned and publicly humiliated him. He had hoped and hoped that she would come back for quite some time. He was prepared to forgive all.

But Diana longed to be dominated by a clever, cruel and unfaithful man. She was entranced with that version of masculinity. I thought this might also be true of Alice de Janzé, then Alice de Trafford, who had fallen so hard for a hard-drinking, gambling brute of a man who mistreated her.

Finally, an edition of *The Green Hat* arrived, and I began to read. There was so much in it. I could quote endlessly. It was a small volume and fitted neatly in my handbag. I carried it with me as a talisman, nestled beside my petite ornate pistol. I read it as Karen Blixen and Denys Finch Hatton would have read their classical poetry. Idina was described in glowing terms. Not only her physical beauty but her presence and her inner core. I felt very shallow and brittle in comparison. I looked at my poor attempts to devise this autobiography and the plain writing style and wondered whether I might steal some phrases and words and insert them into the everyday language.

Beyond the wonderful descriptions of Iris or Idina, the prose did wander off, and I found it hard to follow. Still, I must record some of the amazing phrases: her eyes are described as 'blazing blue, two spoonfuls of the Mediterranean in the early morning of a brilliant day', her hair 'dancing a tawny formal dance about the small white cheeks', 'a jewel of a smile', 'a gallant lady', and she walked 'impersonally, in the fires of herself'. I could not imagine anyone describing me in these terms. I was a crude caricature of a woman when compared to this vision presented in such intellectual terms by Michael Arlen.

In 1950 my personal social life took a surprising turn. Aly Khan, the playboy son of the Aga Khan came to Kenya with his wife, the very famous Hollywood movie star, Rita Hayworth. The purpose of their visit was to see the Ishmaili Muslims. The Aga Khan was their Imam, regarded by them as a man who had a direct link to God.

They were to stay with the Delameres for a night and Tom asked Gilbert and me if he could play host at Oserian, which was a much grander venue than his own property, Soysambu. Gilbert referred the request to me, and I was intrigued. I had met Tom Delamere several times since he and his wife had returned to Kenya. I readily agreed to the proposal and began to make arrangements for such important and glamorous guests. Gilbert had said that he needed to go up to Laikipia to attend to some important cattle business. I didn't mind at all. Mary, Tom's wife, swept in to talk to me about organising the visit. I hadn't met her before, and I must admit I didn't warm to her. The feeling was obviously mutual. She issued her instructions, and I began to feel as if I were a mere lowly housekeeper.

Of course, I had heard of the Aga Khan but I found myself at a loss when it came to who he actually was. I had thought vaguely that he was a royal prince or king in the Middle East. I did some research and found out that he was a member of feudal Indian royalty, born in Karachi. At the age of eight he became the third Aga Khan and forty-eighth Imam. He was a direct descendant of the Prophet, through his daughter, Fatima. He was the world leader of the Nizari Ismailis, the second-largest branch of Shia Muslims, but he had no geographical kingdom. He had fifteen million followers in twenty-five countries. He was regarded as a divine personage. All Ismailis contributed one tenth of their income to their Imam. This comprised an income of hundreds of millions of dollars a year. He was responsible for the welfare of his followers and spent much of his time touring the world visiting them and distributing financial assistance where it was needed.

The Aga's son, Aly, was the heir apparent. He was undoubtedly a playboy but also a very good jockey and he had a keen eye for horses. He and his father loved their racing and they won innumerable Class One races. It was this point that I found interesting. My love of horses had developed in recent years with a string of racehorses, and it was an interest that I shared with Tom Delamere.

The famous couple arrived, and Rita was undoubtedly one of the most beautiful women in the world. She had perfectly formed features, a crown of glorious golden auburn hair and moved like a dancer. Her body seemed to float through the air. Unfortunately, her manifest discontent detracted from her ethereal beauty. She was clearly unhappy with Aly and her complaints ranged from his playboy behaviour to his extravagant spending of her money, which she had earned through her Hollywood films.

They had attended a Cairo New Year's Eve party before flying into Nairobi. Aly confided to Tom that Rita had stormed out of the celebration in one of her famous rages. She and I got on well and I was fascinated to gain a peek into her personal life. She was missing her young child, Yasmin's first birthday because she had agreed to this trip with Aly. She was surprisingly lacking in self-confidence, and was very nervous of meeting the wives of the Ismaili groups. She could not understand their language. Tentatively, I suggested that she might stay behind when Aly made his obligatory trips to meet the religious and she fell upon this idea avidly.

I sometimes wondered how much my suggestion had contributed to the final act in their unhappy marriage. After Aly had departed Tom drove Rita down to Nairobi. She then sent a note to Aly saying that she was returning to Cannes and was going to take the children back to America. He sped down to Nairobi and she agreed that she would return to

Château de l'Horizon and would wait for his return before she went to the United States.

Rita did not keep her word. She packed and took the children to Paris and from there she boarded a liner from Le Havre, bound for New York. Aly was alerted by servants at the Château and chartered a plane and headed to France. He was too late. Rita and the children were bound for America. To make certain that there was no return Rita had announced to journalists that she was leaving her husband and taking her children to the United States.

Aly flew to California and with his charm and silver tongue he did effect a temporary reconciliation, but it didn't last. The marriage was at an end. A curious domino effect could often be observed in the matter of marriage breakups and this event leading to the divorce of the Khans foreshadowed the ending of Gilbert and my union.

Chapter Twelve - The Mau Mau Years

By 1948 there was increasing tension with 220,000 Kikuyu, nearly one-quarter of the Kikuyu population working on white-owned farms in the Highlands. But, increasing use of modern methods meant less labour demand, and farmers were forcing natives off their land back to the reserve or Nairobi. In the background, anti-European 'oathing' had begun.

The black Africans who were politically active had some small success in terms of political representation. In 1950, local government was reconstituted as 33 African district councils with revenue from taxation, property leases and forestry royalties. They were responsible for government roads, health, water, education and agricultural extension. But the situation was worsening at a much faster rate than these small steps forward. The British King announced Nairobi to be a city. Due to increasing landlessness in the rural areas, there were rising prices, overcrowded living conditions, unemployment and crime. Kikuyu gangs and trade unionists controlled many areas of Nairobi. There was a convergence of squatters, the poor in the Central Provinces and Nairobi activists. By 1951 there was a developing underground network between Nairobi's criminal and disaffected underclass, trade unions, and the remnants of

KAU. Mass oathing was now a native form of swearing allegiance to the cause of regaining their lands.

We only heard of the Mau Mau in 1948, which became the term used to refer to the growing anarchy. The white people in Kenya could not make a logical connection between growing unrest amongst the blacks and their legitimate concerns about no legal rights to land ownership. Colonialism was deeply entrenched in the European mindset. There was no awareness that white superiority over the natives was wrong. They just assumed it was the way things were and had always been.

Through the early 1950s, the situation worsened. Trade unions organised numerous general strikes in conjunction with mass oathing. European cattle were mutilated, fires started, a few Europeans were murdered, and black oath-resistors were also killed. Despite this, the Governor, Sir Philip Mitchell, believed there was no serious risk of insurrection. The police tried restoring order through curfews and mass arrests and built a network of informers. Their reaction was to suppress the violence rather than recognise its reasons. Jomo Kenyatta was walking a thin line between violent and non-violent action.

Gilbert and I lived closer to the blacks than most white settlers, and we were more conscious of the growing unrest. Gilbert had taught me to see things from the natives' point of view. I understood that change was inevitable, but I didn't recognise the urgency.

After the war, social upheaval raged around the world, and some liberal-minded white people believed that black Africans should have a say in how their world was organised. One small example of this was the Capricorn Africa Society, started up by Colonel David Stirling. He had fought bravely in the war as leader of the long-range desert group that operated behind enemy lines in North Africa. Elizabeth Powys, a well-known personality in Kenya, strongly supported this movement. She and her husband Will owned 83,000 acres on three separate farms.

This Society tried to put into practice the ideal of multi-racialism. Its basic tenet was 'equal rights for all civilised men.' The definition of 'civilised men' was a minimum degree of education, or ownership of property, or several years of public service. The principle was one of meritocracy. The society had started in Rhodesia and had branches in Nairobi, Dar es Salaam and London. However, black Africans were not interested. They were suspicious of white do-gooders, and they wanted power all to themselves.

As the unrest was brewing, the whites underestimated the ability of the black people to take action. Just as they had not considered a black African assassinating a man like Joss, who was viewed as a threat. Sir Philip Mitchell just wasn't up to snuff. He brushed aside warnings of the impending crisis.

The Mau Mau uprising began in 1952 and lasted three years. Their first publicly recognised action was shooting dead Kiambu Senior Chief Waruhiu wa Kungu, a prominent Christian anti-Mau Mau leader. Sir Evelyn Baring, the recently appointed Governor, called a State of Emergency. The government arrested more than 180 political leaders and deployed a battalion of British soldiers. Most African newspapers were banned.

It was an unstructured revolt against foreign rule, land alienation and political and economic inequality. It had been brewing for at least five years before it became officially recognised. Both parties believed they had right on their side. The British thought they would put down the revolt in a very short time, but it became a guerrilla and civil war.

Most of the conflict was in the northern Kikuyu districts of Nyeri and Fort Hall and the dense bush of the Aberdares. The settlers could not grasp the nature of the enemy. The Mau Mau relied on personal and clan alliances. The British did not consider trying to solve the problems that had caused this situation. The whites believed it was a revolt by an African terrorist movement rooted in black magic. The situation escalated, more extreme oaths were sworn, and there were reports of bestiality and cannibalism.

The Mau Mau disappeared into the mountains in the dense forest of the Aberdares and Kipipiri during the day and came out at night to attack farms. A lot of farmers took on Maasai guards. The Maasai and the Kikuyu had been enemies for years. In 1953 Jomo Kenyatta, who had been arrested, was sentenced to fifteen years in prison. A lot of people were removed from their villages and put in transit camps at Nakuru and Gilgil. They were kept in squalid and overcrowded conditions.

We were living at Naivasha in the early years of the Mau Mau. The police raided us and took away all our staff, leaving only the Muslims. I invited the neighbours and their children to live with us, and they stayed for five months. Even then, people accused me of having an affair with the husband. One District Commissioner has reported that Gilbert's place was crawling with very subversive fellows. The government tried to pin something on him, but he hired an expensive Indian lawyer in Nairobi and was acquitted.

In the midst of the Mau Mau, I had my own personal drama going on. Gilbert had cared for me in those difficult years when I struggled alone with the aftermath of my horrible experience of the murder, the events of the trial, going to Ceylon with Jock, his suicide, the rejection of Nairobi society, the death of my baby and the subsequent miscarriages. It had all been emotionally exhausting. When I finally understood the murder, it brought me a measure of peace. How ironic that this happened at the time of the civil war, and then in the midst of it all, I fell in love again. Even more ironic, it should be Tom Delamere, one of Gilbert's best friends.

I think that the experience of hosting Aly Khan and Rita Hayworth had opened a new vista to me. Rather then the homespun charms of managing herds of cattle on the African plains I had glimpsed the glamorous world of the international jetsetters who rarely spent more than a week or two in any one location. I remembered visiting the south of France when my pearls had been stolen from the glove box. During that trip we had stayed in hotels rather than staying in other people's villas. Aly Khan's description of Château de l'Horizon had entranced me. He had offered that we should come and visit whenever we wished, and I longed to become part of that glamorous world. I was loyal to Gilbert, but I knew that he would never fit in with such people, unlike Tom.

In retrospect, I could have travelled to France on my own and mixed with that crowd, but somehow the idea of being accompanied by Tom Delamere was far more attractive. We had formed a bond during the Khan's visit, and this had grown stronger through our love of horseracing. We had joint ownership of a number of good horses and would attend race days together.

Chapter Thirteen – The Next Husband

Thomas Pitt Hamilton Cholmondeley, 4th Baron Delamere, was conceived in Kenya but born on 19th August 1900 at the family's ancestral estate, Vale Royal in Cheshire. When he was two years old, his father, Lord Delamere, took the family back to Kenya. For many years they lived in very primitive conditions at Elmenteita. During his teenage years, Tom was sent away to Eton

He and his father never got on. They had a major disagreement about selling the last of the Vale Royal estate in Cheshire. Dee had refused to listen to Tom's views about keeping the English property. Beryl Markham told the story that at one point, Dee had thrown a pot of hot tea at Tom, saying, 'How did I ever come to father that?' Tom wasn't keen on Dee's great Kenyan project. He had no heart for it. So, as a young man, he returned to England and joined the Grenadier Guards. Later, he was posted to the Welsh Guards as a junior subaltern.

In 1924 he married Phyllis Scott, the daughter of the 6th Duke of Buccleuch and Lady Elizabeth Manners, the daughter of the 7th Duke of Rutland. She was Lord Francis Scott's niece, one of the highly-placed Kenyan settlers. Their marriage was probably not destined for success when you considered that Tom was short and his new wife, who always wore high heels, towered over him. She was more than six feet tall. Tom's father didn't bother to attend the wedding. He was off visiting southern Africa, promoting the interests of Kenya. The following year, Tom took his new wife to visit Soysambu at Elmenteita. His daughter, Elizabeth, was born on that occasion.

Although the Delamere family was broke, Dee insisted on lavish entertaining when he wanted to impress others with his grand schemes. He once held a dinner for 250 people who drank 600 bottles of champagne. He was pursuing his ongoing mission to promote Kenya, and he thought that such entertaining would aid the cause. In 1927 Tom's second daughter, Anne, was born.

Tom was in Kenya in 1928 when Dee's engagement to Gwladys Markham was announced. Gwladys was twenty-seven years younger than Dee. In the following years, the Delamere estates were in dire financial straits. Dee was generous, had promoted and paid for so many grand schemes that never came off, and had lost all the family money.

By1931, when Dee died of a heart attack, aged only 61 years old, Tom and his family had returned to England. Tom now inherited the title and became Lord Delamere. He didn't have time to return for his father's funeral. However, he had to consider the £226,000 debt his father had left behind. In today's money, this was many millions. For the next fifteen years, Soysambu was in receivership.

In 1934 Tom's wife finally produced a son who was to be his heir. He was born in Queensgate Terrace, in a house belonging to the Duke of Buccleuch. At that time, Tom was working for Everet Jones, an advertising agency and in 1938 became a partner. They pioneered a completely new and very successful pictorial approach to advertising.

A year after Tom's son, Hugh, was born, they moved into the old family home, Vale Royal. When war broke out, they were forced to leave, and the Government converted it into a sanatorium for injured soldiers. Tom rejoined the Welsh Guards. Phyllis and the children went to live in Roxboroughshire with her father. Tom had no money to give Phyllis, and her father had only £1,000 a year to live on. At this stage, when Tom's first marriage went off the rails, Phyllis discovered a liking for Polish soldiers.

Tom divorced Phyllis in 1944 and married the Hon. Ruth Mary Clarisse Ashley. She was already twice divorced but was most famous for being the younger sister of Edwina Mountbatten, the wife of Lord Louis. Tom's second wife was always called Mary, not Ruth. Her mother had died of tuberculosis when she was only five years old, and she grew up at the famous estate, Broadlands, deprived of maternal affection and influence. Her father was a remote figure, busy with his parliamentary career.

Mary was wilful as a child and had symptoms of manic-depression from her teenage years. In 1925 she fell in love with her father's parliamentary private secretary, Alec 'Bobby' Cunningham-Reid. He was a tall man with a pencil-thin moustache and matinee idol looks, a godson of Lord Baden Powell. He had been a flying ace in the Royal Army Corps and was the flying instructor of the Prince of Wales and the Duke of York. Mary's family were concerned about fortune hunters, and she was made a ward of the court to prevent her from marrying Alec, and they were forced to agree not to see each other for a year. Mary became very angry and paranoid and smashed up furniture and accused a family guest of being a disguised brain specialist. She had to be nursed at Adsdean and then sent to a sanatorium in Italy. Eventually, the family relented and allowed the marriage to take place, she was twenty years old, and he was a Conservative MP. The press described them as the richest girl in the world, marrying the most handsome man.

Mary signed over half of her extensive wealth to her husband as she wanted a marriage on equal terms. They lived at one of the family estates, The Hall at Six Mile Bottom, near Newmarket. Mary had two sons and lived in luxury on their 8,000 acre estate. They socialised with the likes of Laurence Olivier, Vivien Leigh and Neville Chamberlain. However, Bobby was serially unfaithful, and eventually, they divorced in 1939. Mary attempted to claw back some of the marriage settlement she had bestowed upon her husband, and they went to court. He was the first man to be granted £10,000 alimony per year. He was also given a house in Upper Brook Street and a yacht.

Mary married again to Major Ernest Laurie Gardner. That lasted only three years. In 1944 Tom divorced Phyllis and immediately married Mary. She was Jewish, red-headed and as mad as a cuckoo. One of her closest friends was Barbara Mcorkindale, who became Barbara Cartland. Tom and Mary moved to Mary's family home at Six-Mile Bottom near Cambridge while living in England before returning to Soysambu after the war.

Tom had two step-sons. Michael Cunningham-Read, who later became a hotelier in Kenya and the first non-national to be granted a Kenyan passport. Noel Cunningham-Read became a racing driver. He had good relationships with both of them. Perhaps, better than his relationship with his son and heir, Hugh.

The war years proved profitable for Kenya. In the early 1950s, Tom received a notification from the bank that the overdraft had been paid off, and they were not asking for payment of the interest due to his father's services to the country. He made the momentous decision to return to Kenya. He became a member of Muthaiga and also a steward of the Jockey Club. His advertising agency was sold for a handsome profit to Bensons. Later, it became Saatchi and Saatchi. Mary insisted that she take her Jersey cows to East Africa. Tom decided to cut his ties with England and sold Vale Royal for a pittance to the chemical company ICI Ltd. Soysambu now entered a time of prosperity. Tom was employing eight European managers.

Michael Cunningham-Reid, one of Mary's sons, arrived in Kenya, where he was meant to take up a job as a farm hand for £10 a month. He lasted only one day and then returned to Soysambu. Tom was not pleased and promptly despatched him to another property, Ol Pejeta, to work with Robin Long (son of Boy Long) under Gerald Southey's manager. He didn't last long there either and eventually returned to live at Sugonoi House at Soysambu. Eventually, Boy Long, living alone on the homestead, died, and Tom and Mary moved into what was then called Main House.

Mary organised some renovations to improve it. It was certainly not grand in those days. Tom's father was famous for his lack of attention to comfortable living. Mary had a wing built on with a veranda, and bathrooms were added. Mary then decided that her son, Michael, needed his own property and her trustees paid for the 800 acre Spring Farm, situated on the escarpment behind Sugonoi House.

Mary had been mentally unstable long before she had married Tom. She would throw tremendous tantrums and descend into the depths of depression that affected everyone in the household. Tom didn't know how to cope and adopted the fallback position of a stiff upper lip, which only made it worse.

In February 1952, the Duke and Duchess of Edinburgh arrived in Kenya. There were great processions in Nairobi and a garden party at Government House. The royal majesties then went to Nyeri. The Duke played polo and they stayed the night at Treetops. This is a famous miniature hotel built in the fork of a huge 300-year-old fig tree. It was built over a large waterhole, the edges of which formed a natural salt lick. It is a remote spot on an elephant migration path to Mt Kenya. To get to the hotel, you must walk the last quarter mile on a track that the animals also use to go to the waterhole. As there is a danger that guests might come across a rhino, buffalo or elephant, there are wooden ladders nailed to trees along the way so one can climb to safety.

When they arrived in the hotel branches, they found that the baboons had raided the toilet and festooned the place with toilet paper. All night the Duke and Duchess and their staff of two, Pammy, the daughter of Edwina Mountbatten, who was acting as lady-in-waiting and a young Australian, Mike Parker, stayed awake to watch the parade of wild animals visiting the waterhole. On that night, King George VI died.

However, the Queen was blissfully unaware of this. Although messages were sent by cypher to Nairobi, the Governor had taken the cypher book with him to Mombasa, where the royal party were to embark. The resident hunter, Jim Corbett, wrote in the register that it was the first time a Princess ascended a tree and a Queen descended.

Inevitably, I fell to thinking how I would have attended the Coronation of Queen Elizabeth as a Countess if Joss had not died, and we had married and stayed together. Looking back, I think this might have spurred me to pursue more than a close friendship with Tom. We had become joint racehorse owners, which was rather threatening for poor Mary. She had divined our close relationship. Gilbert was very good friends with Tom, and the three of us spent a lot of time together. Mary was the odd one out.

Tom, like Joss, was a brilliant bridge player, but he had no academic education, and he resented his son, Hugh's success in that area. Hugh was also much taller than Tom, which was another reason for conflict between them. Tom was conscious of his short stature, which had blighted his first marriage to Phyllis.

As I have written in the previous chapter, the Mau Mau rebellion began in 1952. In that same year, Beryl Markham returned from the United States. She had hoped that she might work for Tom. However, Mary knew about their history when Beryl had initiated a teenage Tom into the joys of sex. She raised vociferous objections. As a result, Beryl moved into someone else's guest house and re-established herself as a racehorse trainer. Mary wasn't keen on Beryl, but she was insanely jealous of my friendship with Tom and our shared interest in racehorses.

In saying that Mary was 'insane', I'm not overstating the case. When she did finally leave Tom and divorced him, and returned to England, Edwina tried to have her certified and committed to a psychiatric institution. Mary's two sons, Michael and Tom, stood up for her, and it was agreed that she should live at Six Mile Bottom and have regular treatment at the Midhurst mental institution.

But here I am leaping ahead of the sequence of events. It was all happening at once. Tom was surprisingly anti-war, and he was all for the independence of Kenya. Many other white settlers did not agree with his stance on the matter. Gilbert didn't say much, but he did spend his days with his pack of hunting dogs, Dobermans and Labradors, chasing down terrorists. In comparison, Tom was Chairman of the Employer's Association, and he protected his staff during the Emergency and didn't allow them to go into detention. It was rumoured that oath-taking took place in Sugonoi House. Tom always denied any knowledge of this activity.

In the middle of the rebellion, Tom's son, Hugh, returned to Kenya. He had been studying in England. Tom wouldn't employ him as a manager, so Gilbert gave him six months' work. That year, I made my decision. I would leave Gilbert and marry Tom. I wasn't 'running away. I made sure not to act like a Bolter. I was moving on with my life in a considered and calculating way. Although Gilbert was richer than Tom, he didn't have a title. I cannot entirely deny the charge of being scheming. I had given the matter careful thought and was fairly certain I could manage it, and we could all stay friends. Of course, that didn't include Mary. Inevitably, someone always gets hurt. In a relationship, one always loves more than the other. Gilbert loved me more than I loved him, and Tom certainly didn't care much for Mary. She had tried his patience for too many years with her tantrums and mad moods. I didn't like to speculate who would love more between Tom and myself.

I certainly felt passion for him. Not exactly in the same way as I had felt for Joss. I was a different woman in my forties. More than twelve years after Joss's death, I had gone through miscarriages and now had a beautiful adopted daughter. I was more mature and had been acting out the role of a good wife for many years. I had trained myself for this, and the added layer of attraction and sexual interest, not to mention the lure of a title, meant that I had no problems managing our marriage.

You probably remember my glamorous young mother, with her older husband, who lived in a *ménage à trois*. Inevitably, one followed in the course of past family life. Although I don't think darling Snoo will be physically close to Gilbert as I was with my father. Poor Gilbert didn't have that much imagination. Only when it came to his handsome, exotic young Maasai men.

One of the changes that had to be negotiated was moving from Oserian to Soysambu. There was no house in Kenya as grand as Oserian. Although it was still in my name, I couldn't expect Tom to live there. At least my lifestyle would change with Tom, and I could entertain much more. Poor Gilbert was decidedly anti-social and nobly suffered whenever we had guests.

Soysambu was a ranch in the Rift Valley. The sprawling one-storey house was on top of a ridge overlooking the lake, and there was a belt of tall umbrella thorn trees surrounding it. The countryside around the alkaline Lake Elmenteita was very different to Lake Naivasha. The shoreline consisted of low craggy hills covered in acacias. There were mobs of rose-pink flamingos, a variety of waterfowl and breeding pelicans on the rocky island in the middle of the lake. They spiralled up the air thermals in the morning and flew to the neighbouring Lake Nakuru to feed.

Fresh morning air, endless savannah, plains stretching for miles around, and in the distance mountains were scoured by ravines and ridged with forest. Chilly mysterious dawn, ribbons of pearly mist lying in the gullies and the giant bulk of the mountains in the distance, as the sun came up it flooded the plains. Riding out in the early morning, the weaver birds chattered, the boubou shrikes sounded their bell-like notes, and iridescent starlings hopped across the boughs of the acacia trees.

I didn't dither and flap about the change in husband. I weighed up the situation, and I made the best decision. I had grown into a calm and purposeful woman. Tom and I had been flirting with each other almost since the first day that we had met. Gilbert pretended not to notice. Mary glowered at us. I think all the danger and excitement of the Mau Mau, the blood lust and the fight for one's land and livelihood were a force that carried us along. Life with Gilbert was safe, and he cared for me, but I longed for some sexual excitement. I wanted to be Diana, Lady Delamere. Looking back from the late seventies, this doesn't seem as important, but in those days, especially in Kenya, a title meant something. I had been Lady Delves Broughton and losing that had been a blow. Besides, the name Delamere certainly carried some weight in East Africa.

Tom was surprisingly ardent, and for a small man, he was well-endowed. It reminded me, just a little, of my first days with Joss, who was famed as a demon lover. Tom's first wife, Phyllis, was said to have been very sexually orientated with her string of Polish military men. Tom must have learnt a trick or two from her.

I had worked carefully on maintaining our cosy threesome. I had devised related animal soubriquets. I was Little White Bear, Tom was Little Brown Bear, and Gilbert was Poo Bear, or Pooey.

Mary divorced Tom, citing me as co-respondent. She had always hated me and referred to me as the murderess, waging a campaign against me since our first meeting. She would tell stories of her family, particularly the grand connections of her sister, Edwina, through her marriage to Dicky Mountbatten. There were many photographs in silver frames placed around the house, and several were of the Mountbattens' wedding at St Margaret's, the church beside Westminster Abbey, in July 1922. Of course, like the rest of the population of England, I had been aware of the wedding. I was nine years old. Mary had been a bridesmaid, and none of us was allowed to forget it. A crowd of at least 8,000 people was watching from the streets. The Star had cited it as the Wedding of the Century. Dickie was a member of the extended Royal Family, and the Prince of Wales was the best man. The bridal car was a Rolls-Royce drawn by a naval gun crew around Parliament Square, and then a flag-draped lorry took over and towed the car past Buckingham Palace to the reception at Brook House in Park Lane. The wedding cake was so enormous that it took four men to lift it. It had a top tier shaped like a crown, plus miniature anchors, sails and hawsers with tiny lifeboats hanging from silver davits.

Dicky, Mary's brother-in-law, was the brother of Prince Philip's mother. So, they were all related to European royalty, and the connections were very complicated, but Mary insisted on detailing the various relationships.

Then, there were also photos of Patricia Mountbatten's wedding, which had taken place at the end of the war before Tom and Mary returned to Kenya. This wedding was not quite as grand but had caused a furore when Prince Philip had betrayed his intimate relationship with Princess Elizabeth when he had casually taken her coat from her. The newspapers made much of this, and Mary, who probably didn't care much for her niece, droned on and on about it.

I had no similar stories of royal connection. My only claim to such fame was being married to Sir Delves Broughton and having an affair with Lord Erroll, which ended in shame and disgrace. My marriage to Gilbert Colvile, in spite of being one of the richest men in Kenya, cut no ice. My defence in the face of this shameless boasting of aristocratic connections was to feign interest and adopt a suitably fawning interest. As I put on this performance, Tom would look at me with a glint in his eye, and it was all we could do not to guffaw with laughter.

For some reason, Tom's son, Hugh, also disliked me, and there were whispers over the years that he told other people that it was me who had killed Joss. He even elaborated on this story with ridiculous tales of how I had taken pot shots at other men who were my lovers. I don't know how he figured this, but it was probably jealousy that his father adored me and didn't rate him at all. Tom thought he was useless. Just as the previous Lord Delamere had been cruel to Tom, so Tom was cruel to Hugh.

Gilbert moved into his shepherd's hut, returning to his old ways of plain, simple living. He had changed his lifestyle a lot for my sake, but now he was happy to go back to living like the Maasai. He was sad in some ways that we were to be divorced, but he had always found my love of luxury a little irksome. Tom and I set up a special set of rooms for him at Soysambu so he could come and stay whenever he wanted.

Tom announced our engagement at the Nakuru races that November. I remember the moment well. The hotels were filled, the streets humming, and the modest grandstand blazing with a patchwork of coloured finery donned by men and women whose hearts were light with the joy of meeting their friends, drinking – a rest from the drudgery of farming and wresting a living from this land.

I especially remember the gasps of astonishment that greeted this announcement. I knew that no one had expected me to marry Gilbert and this progression to Tom seemed like a logical step to me. Obviously, not to the racegoers who were buzzing at the news. They came up to congratulate us, but their smirks belied their words. I wondered if anyone there was at all genuinely happy for us.

I suppose they were all saying that I was marrying Tom for his title, and he was marrying me for all the money and property that Gilbert had given me. There is always a little truth in the spiteful judgements of others. But, if you think about it, Mary was an heiress with a huge trust fund, much richer than me. So, Tom was giving up his access to her money by marrying me. But, on the other hand, I was efficient and reasonable. I was good at getting what I wanted with tact and charm. I had accepted the tenet that it is easier to catch flies with honey.

During that golden transition time between the announcement of our engagement and our marriage, Tom escorted me into the Muthaiga Club. I returned in triumph to this bastion of the Kenyan socialites and gloried in every minute of it. There was the usual tranche of tall, slim, elegant young lovelies, but I was the living legend, the infamous Diana Delves Broughton, about to become Diana, Lady Delamere. The comfortable chintzy rooms looked the same as when I had first arrived in 1940. Now, there was the addition of a swimming pool. I couldn't wait to lounge beside it in my latest chic swimming costume. Undoubtedly, the menu in the dining room would include the old favourites such as toad in the hole, fish pie followed by bread and butter pudding with the added piquancy of traditional English marmalade or treacle tart and custard or cream.

Tom and I married on the 26th March 1955. Our friend Marcus Wickham-Boynton was the best man. I was only forty-two years old and was still looking rather good. Tom was fifty-five. I remember feeling a sense of complete happiness, that all was right with the world during the ceremony. I had come full circle and mastered the vagaries of fate and the men who loved me wanted nothing but my happiness. It was strange to think that if Gwladys had lived, she would have been my stepmother-in law How convoluted were relationships in the small community in Kenya!

There was a wave of titillating gossip when Gilbert came with us on our honeymoon to England. We did have a jolly time and were all at ease with the situation. We went to the races and looked around for new horses to send back to Kenya. We dined in the best restaurants in London. I'm not sure that Gilbert liked England much. I'm sure he was thinking longingly of his cows and the Maasai and couldn't wait to return.

We got back to Kenya, and there was the ongoing drama of the Mau Mau. Gilbert sent Maasai guards to keep us safe. However, he still accompanied Tom and me to the races, and we remained a friendly trio. If nothing else, one could say that I was good at managing the men in my life.

Eventually, in October 1956, the war ended with the capture and execution of Kimathi. However, some rebels remained in the mountains. Sporadic attacks occurred until Independence. The tally of deaths was at least 14,000 black Africans, 29 Asians and 95 Europeans. Kikuyu suspects had been frequently beaten and tortured. Between 150,000 and 320,000 had been detained for varying lengths of time in over 50 detention camps. Treatment in the camps, by mainly untrained staff, was brutal, using forced confessions, beating, and the inculcation of so-called 'Christian values.'

The truth came out later that in the trial of Kenyatta, the government had bribed a witness to make false statements, and the British judge was given £20,000 to facilitate a conviction. So much for the British justice system!

In 1954 the controversial Swynnerton Plan was implemented. It meant that previously communal-owned land was given individual title, giving the Kikuyu a headstart in a rush for land ownership. This was a form of divide and rule, with some black Africans owning the land and others rendered landless labourers.

Chapter Fourteen – Living at Soysambu

Our married life was comfortably established at Soysambu, living in some style but not ostentatiously. The house did not have the elegance of Oserian. The servants were dressed in long khaki tunics with green cummerbunds and trousers. At Kilifi, the servants dressed in plain white and the boys who worked on the boat wore navy-blue drill shorts or trousers and matching t-shirts. The name of my boat, *White Bear,* was embroidered on the t-shirts.

I did my best to institute some civilised customs. Breakfasts were always served in bedrooms, and guests were given printed menu cards at dinner. Guests had to tick their preferences, whether it was tropical fruits or cooked dishes.

I commissioned many changes. The back patio was covered in a stylish pattern of black and white tiles. The front drawing-room was added with the best view that was available. I never grew tired of looking down at the lake with the myriad of birds there. Whenever I went away, I loved to return to the evocative soft smell of soda.

I had a silver bear fitted on the bonnet of our Mercedes. Tom, like Joss, didn't shoot. He was a raconteur, very entertaining, and fun. This made up for the fact that he wasn't handsome, rather short and dumpy, with unattractive sandy ginger hair. As I got older, my social allure was heightened in my new circumstances, and I seemed always to have a string of hangers-on. It wasn't that I was particularly fond of them, but I think that wealth and glamour do attract people. They hope that by hanging around me, it might rub off on them. It did make me feel more secure after that time in the forties when no one had wanted to be associated with me.

Every last Saturday of every month, we had a grand lunch at Soysambu. I would have smoked salmon, champagne, guinea fowl, and lots of puddings – puddings are always so important. They are the mark of luxury when one lives with bare necessities and spends most evenings chewing on the bones of something that has been recently shot. Pink gin was the standard tipple in Kenya; gallons of it were drunk at these meals. I loved being the hostess presiding over this sort of event. I had finally found my element.

Tom did have his demons. He had almost two distinct personalities. Especially with Hugh, he would be dictatorial, arrogant and foul-tempered, but he never treated me like that. He was always tolerant, caring and gracious. He hadn't been treated well by his own father, which was ironic as the previous Lord Delamere was known to be helpful and kind to so many people. Just not to his own son.

Lady Patricia Fairweather, one of my friends, had a cottage built nearby so we could be close to each other. Many people thought we had a lesbian relationship, and again, I will state emphatically that I was not interested in sexual relationships with other women. Patricia lived near us for fifteen years, and I can tell you that Tom and I were relieved when she finally left. She was an alcoholic and used to set her irascible dog on Tom.

Snoo grew up with dark hair and bronzed skin. She was without affectation, always cheerful and no-nonsense about her. People thought she was nothing like me, but I think she was the type of girl that I would have liked to be if I hadn't been beset with sibling rivalry with my sister and to an extent, with my younger mother. I think that Snoo being an only child was a blessing for her. She got all my attention, not only a partial distribution amongst brothers and sisters. Tom had an heir so there was no question of having to provide him with a son.

In 1960 Edwina Mountbatten died suddenly of a coronary artery thrombosis when she was visiting Borneo. There was a huge hullabaloo over her death, and much was written about her in the newspapers. Ever since Tom had divorced Mary to marry me, I had taken a great interest in Edwina Mountbatten and her very unusual marriage to Dickie of the many royal connections.

She became one of the groups of women of that era with whom I was fascinated. Like Diana Mosley, she had not come to Kenya when I lived there, although there was talk that she had once visited Happy Valley in its heyday when she was travelling around with her long-term lover Bunny. The raunchy lives of both Edwina and Dickie put the hedonistic Happy Valleyites in the shade. Both Mountbattens had numerous short-term and long-term affairs. Edwina had a particular penchant for black men, and I thought it was probably best that she hadn't spent much time in Kenya as crossing the white-black divide with sexual relations was, until Independence, considered more scandalous than murder or incest. Lord Mountbatten had been nicknamed Mountbottom in the navy and was known for liking handsome young sailors. What I found fascinating about this marriage was that it survived and that the two of them became closer and more loving towards each other as the years went on.

In the same year that Edwina died, the State of Emergency in Kenya was lifted by the new Governor Patrick Muir Renison. The British Government and Kenyan leaders met in Lancaster House in London, and the date for Independence was set in 1963. There was to be a mixed-race government. The World Bank instituted a willing buyer-willing seller scheme to redistribute land, so there was a more equitable distribution to the black Africans. Administration jobs that had previously only been available for whites opened up to employ black people.

Decolonisation took place in the three years from 1960 until 1963. Then, there were anti-colonial 'winds of change', Cold War undercurrents, settlers' fear that they would lose their land and always the black Africans' relentless desire for the return of their land.

Statistics are helpful in understanding Kenyan society at that time. In 1962 the population was 8.6 million people, and most of these people were living an agricultural or pastoral life. The average life expectancy was 35, and half of the population was under 16 years. The Kikuyu constituted 19% of the population, the once-powerful Maasi less than 2%, and the Europeans less than 1%.

Tom was the President of the Kenya Farmer's Union. At the opening of the 15th Annual Meeting, he stated that no one would want to return to the White Highlands of the past. I felt a passing qualm as I remembered how Joss had so passionately believed that the Highlands be reserved for the white people. The days of Happy Valley would never return. Everyone was talking about the Settlement Scheme, Land Bank Finance and setting up an Agricultural Credit Organisation.

Governor Patrick Renison and his wife came to visit, and they brought their young daughter Ann. She was twenty-two years old and had already married and separated from her first husband. At first, I was annoyed that I had one extra guest. It ruined my numbers. Two extra chairs had to be included at the dining table, which had been set for eight. I was very particular about my social arrangements and hated impromptu changes. Hugh was roped in as an extra man. Then, I got over my fit of anger and began to take an interest in this young woman.

She had been born in Ceylon when her father had been Private Secretary to the Governor. Her mother had been a Gibb and was a cousin of Alistair Gibb, who had been the love of Gwladys, the one she had loved and languished over at the time of Joss's murder.

Ann's parents had later moved from Ceylon to Trinidad and Tobago and, after that, Honduras. Ann had been sent back to England to school and had spent many holidays with her cousins. When she was twenty, she joined her parents in British Guyana. That was when she had married a sugar farmer called Michael Tinne, an old Etonian. She explained this decision as there wasn't much else to do. When she left him, she joined her parents in Kenya and began working for a Greek herpetologist, Constantine Ionides. He sent her all over Kenya to collect poisonous snakes.

Ann was not classically beautiful, petite with a cute, little button nose. Her crowning glory was masses of long red-brown hair and unusual green eyes. Tom and I were determined that she would make a good wife for Hugh, who was seeing a most unsuitable young woman at the time. Ann was well-bred and well-travelled. After tea, we went for a walk, and I sent Hugh and Ann down a separate road alone. My machinations worked, and they fell in love and wanted to marry. There was just the problem of getting Ann divorced. Tom did have some reservations as Ann's family was firmly on the side of the administration, as opposed to settlers, but he got over this with my persuasive arguments that she would do very well for Hugh. Ann's mother had the same reservations. She wasn't keen on the Kenyan aristocracy.

A divorce for Ann had to be arranged, and as Tinne was Scottish, they had to travel there to comply with the stricture that there must be evidence of adultery. Tom paid their fares, and Ann's parents, who were now retired in England, lent them a car. On the 11th of April, 1964, they got married at Main House. There weren't many guests on Hugh and Ann's side, so I had to bolster up the numbers with my own friends. We sent the newlyweds down to the Mnarani Club for their honeymoon. They were water-skiing, and Hugh swerved up onto the beach and broke his toe. I suppose it was eventful rather than romantic.

Bizarrely, Tom's daughter, my step-daughter, had married Sir Evelyn Broughton after the war. Sir Evelyn was the son of Jock, my second husband. They had a flat in Ebury Street in London, near Victoria station. Apparently, they weren't happy, and it was rumoured that Sir Evelyn lacked libido. When you map out human relationships, they get tangled in such a web of connections. Especially in Kenya, the pool of eligible partners was relatively small, and everyone knew everyone. But the tentacles attaching us to England were strong. I wished that there hadn't been this connection. Unaccountably, it made me feel uneasy.

Chapter Fifteen - Independence

In the years leading up to Independence, there were swirling movements of discontent. The black Africans who were released from detention returned to find their assets gone. There were legal and illegal moves afoot. To try and assuage the strong feelings of the black Africans, the Government lifted the ban on black ownership of the Highlands. In saying this, only a tiny number of allies were allowed to take land, and it came under the spurious title of a 'good husbandry' law. I imagined Joss turning in his grave. The white-only Highlands had been one of his core beliefs. It was not a free-for-all for black Africans. They had to be selected based on their capital and their farming experience. Black-owned farms were carefully distributed amongst white-owned farms.

I think this was a deliberate policy as the predominant fear of the white people was that communism would get a grip through the likes of Odinga. It was at the beginning of 1963 that Kim Philby, 'the third man', had run to Moscow when it had become increasingly clear that he was a dyed in-the-wool communist spy. The fact that he had been the head of the anti-communist section of M16 made it all the worse. The Cold War was waging fiercely, and paranoia was rampant.

The political situation at that time was tumultuous. As a white person, you had to decide either to go or to leave. Many chose to go. In the first few months of 1961, 5,586 more Europeans had left than had arrived. I believed that all who departed left something of themselves behind. They lost something integral to their own identities, especially those who had been born in Kenya.

Schools for white Europeans were forced to close. Over a million acres of the seven and a half million acres of land farmed by white settlers were bought to be redistributed. This cost the British Treasury around £12 million. Tom, at the time, believed that only 40% of the white farmers would depart. At the same time, with improved medical treatment and increased food availability, the population of black Kenyans was increasing exponentially.

The gap between the views of Kenyan white settlers and that of the British Government was as wide as ever. The white settlers believed they had been sold out, and the British Government wanted to eliminate their embarrassing situation as a colonial power in Kenya. Delamere Avenue was renamed Kenyatta Avenue. The statue of Delamere was removed and placed at Soysambu. I was privately incensed at this. It had been Joss's initiative that had meant that four years after Lord Delamere's death that it should be named

Delamere Avenue. However, in those tumultuous times, it was best to keep one's opinions to oneself.

Kenyatta was now 73 years old, and he called for forgiveness and forgetting of the past and a positive view of the future. Tom got on very well with Kenyatta, and he asked him to address a meeting at Nakuru Town Hall to speak to over 350 white farmers. He talked about building the nation in a spirit of togetherness which was called *Harambee*. Not many of the white farmers were convinced.

The first true national elections held in 1962 resulted in a previously undreamed of African majority in the Legislative Assembly. There were two major African political parties, the KANU and the KADU. Kenyatta was the leader of the KANU. The main forces that decided allegiance were region and ethnicity. KADU secured the support of the Kalenjin and Maasai, the coastal Mijikenda and sections of the Abaluhya. KANU won 19 seats, KADU won 11, minor parties and independents took the remaining three. As a result, the balance of power of between the KANU and the KADU was held by the minor parties, independents, and the 20 seats reserved for non-Africans, the white, Arab and Asian councillors. I must say I found Kenyan politics very hard to understand and Tom spent considerable time explaining it to me, even drawing diagrams to make it clearer.

On everyone's lips, in every newspaper, on the streets was the word 'Uhuru'. The word comes from the Arabic and Hebrew language, which has been adopted into Swahili and roughly translates as 'freedom' or 'independence'. To the blacks it is Utopia when they will live a life of ease and freedom, unfettered by the chains of European colonisation. To the white Europeans it is a threat. Everything they have worked for in Africa is to be wrest from them. It is an Act of God, *'Shauri ya Mungu'* and no man, white or black will stop it.

On 12th December 1963 Kenya gained independence. On 11th December 200,000 Kenyans witnessed the article of independence being given by the Duke of Edinburgh and Colonial Secretary Duncan Sandys to Jomo Kenyatta. On that chilly night in Nairobi the Union Jack was lowered and the black, green and red flag of Kenya hoisted. Government House was renamed State House. Kenya was one of the last British colonies in Africa to gain independence, and the last in East Africa. It was the dawning of a new world for all of us.

Behind the scenes, on the eve of Independence, the British removed and hid most records of the civil war. They did this in order to protect the loyalists and also themselves from demands for atrocities that had been committed. Ex-Mau

Mau were given no entitlements to land or jobs. Some of the most compromised colonial chiefs were quickly retired.

Much has been written about Kenyatta but some of his actions immediately after Independence have not been highlighted. He was symbolically a King. His photo was in every shop, and he was pictured on the currency. His style was flamboyant. In 1965 he opened the new Kenyan House of Representatives clad in leopard skins. On other occasions his costume combined that of an African chief and a European monarch. He used his skills as a showman and mythmaker to full effect in those early days of Independence. He was a pragmatist rather than an idealist, although he had written along the lines of political philosophy that was not the way he ruled.

He accumulated an extensive personal fortune. As the Prime Minister and the President, he received many gifts. He became notorious for requisitioning goods and had a careless disregard when it came to paying for anything. By 1965, the Kenyatta family owned huge amounts of land. His allies tended to follow his example. Kenyatta oversaw a neo-patrimonial system, rather than a party state. His personal dominance was very powerful.

Europeans now had a chance to take up Kenyan citizenship. Dual citizenship was not an option, so one had to choose whether to be Kenyan or British. Tom and I applied for

Kenyan citizenship with alacrity. Although, we were committed to Kenya, we did send our money to offshore accounts. Tom's son, Hugh also took up Kenyan citizenship. I kept a lot of newspaper clippings of that time and pasted them into scrapbooks. I was very proud of the part that Tom had played in this massive change in the country which we both loved. Tom worked in tandem with another pro-independence white, Bruce McKenzie.

Upon Independence, McKenzie had been appointed Minister of Agriculture and he remained in office throughout the 1960s. He was the only European in the Cabinet. He was a larger-than-life figure with high levels of energy; a hunter, pilot, farmer and politician. He managed settler selection and settlement. By the end of 1965, there were only 1,100 European mixed farmers left. The European population in 1962 was 56,000, and it dramatically decreased to 41,000 by 1969. The population of Asians in 1962 was 180,000, three times that of the Europeans. Many Asians found the equality of Africans difficult to accept. Many lost their jobs as clerks in the civil service after Independence. Most Asians chose not to take up Kenyan nationality, unlike the Arab population who had lived along the coast for generations who did become Kenyan.

Derek Erskine, from whose stables Jock and I had leased riding horses when we first arrived, was an old Etonian, who had arrived in Kenya in the early thirties to work for the Kenya Broadcasting Services, but he had a lisp and could not pronounce his 'r's. Instead, he started up a bakery with his wife Elizabeth and later had a very successful grocery business. He believed passionately in a multi-racial Kenyan society, making him extremely unpopular with most white settlers. Derek fought passionately for the release of Jomo Kenyatta, who had been imprisoned. He had travelled with an African delegation to Lancaster House in London, lobbying for Kenyatta's release. When he had returned to Kenya, a group of angry settlers met him at the airport and thirty pieces of silver was flung at him. Derek was later knighted by the Queen at Kenyatta's request.

Chapter Sixteen – After Independence

I entered a new stage in my social life after Independence. I made a conscious effort to change my ways. I used to go into Nairobi to the Thorn Tree Café to enjoy an iced coffee frothing with ice cream. It was an indulgence and not at all my usual style, which had been firmly mired in the 1930s for so long. It was a token attempt at living like the ordinary people now that Kenya was no longer under British rule. The New Stanley Hotel had a face lift. I also liked to dine at Alan Bobbe's grill restaurant. Finally, I was an accepted figure on the social scene, having paid my dues in those years after Joss's murder. The fickle inhabitants of Nairobi were now happy to know me. I was Lady Delamere, part of the great Delamere dynasty, the closest thing to royalty that we had in Kenya.

I found a group of new Nairobi friends younger than me. They took me along to the Limuru Country Club, which was twenty-five miles north of Nairobi. They told me that Muthaiga was now considered hopelessly old-fashioned, and it was best to be seen at Limuru. I found it so strange that blacks and whites mingled effortlessly in the clubhouse, which resembled what was probably meant to be an old-fashioned British pub. They would take their children to the swimming club, and we sat well back to avoid the splashiness and cheered them on in impromptu races.

The view from the Country Club was spectacular, and my gaze would slip off into the distance. A carpet of springy Kikuyu grass rolled down the undulating slopes. There were carefully cultivated stands of jacaranda and cypress. The clumpy bushes were bright with flowers; pink protea, blue agapanthus, and white datura.

I was even persuaded to go to what was supposedly the most popular restaurant in town called The Carnivore. There was no menu, and you could eat as much as you liked for one hundred Kenyan Shillings. A barbecue pit in the centre of the room had spits on which all sorts of speared meats turned. There was everything you could imagine, from antelope to goat. You were served by Maasi boys dressed in *shukas,* who would bring the meat to your table and hack off a chunk at your request. Side dishes included only salads and garlic bread.

Nairobi was changing. The white Europeans and Asians lost their jobs in the civil service. Those posts nearly all went to black Africans. But many countries rushed to open embassies in Nairobi, non-government organisations, the World Health Organisation, aid programs, and major charities. Nairobi was considered a plum posting, almost a paid holiday in fully staffed and furnished houses in high-security compounds with duty-free alcohol and a car with a driver. There were whispers that the Cultural Attaché was also working as an Intelligence Officer. This added a dash of intrigue, spicing up the endless round of presentations, charity events, drinks, and dinner parties. It certainly made a welcome change from the stuffy old British matrons and their husbands who previously dominated the social scene that centred around Government House. We had endless fun imagining networks of spies that the Americans and the Israelis were probably running. Then, we identified several Germans or Austrians who we suspected might have been Nazis. This meant an international investigation hobnobbing with friends at home who might have information. It was certainly an interesting and diverting hobby. I carefully turned away from any disturbing private thoughts of Joss and the British Union of Fascists. That was just too far in the past.

Another new social development was inter-racial sexual relationships and, most shockingly, adulterous and illicit relationships. I can't say that this sort of thing didn't go on before, but it was very hush-hush, and discretion was totally necessary. Now, it was out in the open, and for those of us of my generation, it required a conscious effort not to look shocked when the gossip headed that way.

The darker side of the new Kenya was beginning to emerge. As forecast, corruption was casting an increasingly murky shadow as the months ticked by. More sinister was the new arms trade that had become increasingly profitable. There was a need for guns, grenades and worse which were sold to the highest bidder, whether it was the Kenyans who were fighting the *shifta* Somali bandits in the north, the Sudanese Arabs looking at taking over the western regions currently settled by African Christians, or the Hutus in the Congo who hated the Watutsis, the Zanzibari Muslims who were not happy about being ruled by Tanzanian Christians and the Kenyan Luos who still bore a grudge against the Kikuyu who had grabbed so much of the land. In addition, carjacking was becoming prevalent and armed gangs were stealing trucks loaded with coffee coming out of Uganda and Burundi.

Spending time with my girlfriends away from Soysambu gave me time to gird my loins to return to the rather tricky atmosphere at home. Tom was increasingly housebound, and I had plenty to chat to him about, telling him about recent events in Nairobi. I spent considerable time and energy trying to smooth the tempestuous relationship between him and Hugh. Whenever Tom lost his temper at what he viewed as Hugh's stupidity, I tried to point out that Tom might have easily done something like that when he was young. I don't suppose Hugh will remember my efforts.

Somewhere along the line, he had picked up and run with the myth of his 'wicked step-mother'.

Hugh had even spread rumours of me playing around with other men. This was totally untrue. Tom was very strict about monogamy. He didn't want me running around, and I loved him. I had rather lost interest in having sex with random men. I found delight in other things these days, racehorses, entertaining and deep-sea fishing. I also had a keen interest in dog shows, and my pugs were the best in the country. Tom wasn't keen on them, but he humoured me.

Gilbert died of a stroke in 1966. He was seventy-eight years old, which is a respectable age. I don't think that he was adapting well to this new Kenya. He had not been a flexible person. As we buried Gilbert, I thought that it was best that he had gone. Kenyan life had become much more complex than simply husbanding a huge number of cattle to graze on endless acres of privately owned land. Gilbert had been a pioneer to the bone. He had no desire to bend to the cataclysmic changes that were shaking Kenya to her roots. Tom was coping, as I knew he would, because he had lived in England for many years, and he had a flexibility of thought that came from being submerged in different cultures and taking the best from each.

Gilbert was buried at the burial place at *Ndabibi* with the epitaph *'If you want a memorial, look around you'*. My inheritance from Gilbert was in the region of two and a half million pounds. He left everything to me, including his mother's jewels, which would go to Snoo later. He had five separate properties totalling about 265,000 acres. The largest was at Lariak on the Laikipia plains, covering 160,000 acres. Eventually, I decided that it was not wise for a white woman to own so much land in Kenya at those times. It was sold to the Laikipia West Land Buying Company. The land-buying company was fronted by the Laikipia senator and long-serving Laikipia West MP GG Kariuki, an assistant minister in the Jomo Kenyatta government.

In these years, Snoo had finished school in England and did a secretarial course in Nairobi, and then I sent her to Paris to a finishing school. I insisted that she be presented as a debutante so that she could be introduced to society in England. She wasn't keen to say the very least. She had her hair styled in a bouffant which was fashionable at the time but she refused to smile for the cameras. She declared that all the eligible young men that she met were nothing but chinless wonders.

When she was twenty-one, she married an army man in England. We didn't go to the wedding, which was a very small-scale affair, celebrated with cups of tea rather than champagne. Tom and I hadn't approved of the match, and later, Snoo admitted that it was a ridiculous act of rebellion.

She was married for only three years, and her husband, Mr Moorehead, was openly unfaithful. I found this all rather hard to bear, I had wanted so much for Snoo not to make my own mistakes, but it seems that nothing you say can make your child live a perfect life.

Tom and I continued to share our passion for horse racing, and there is a famous photograph of me being presented with the silver trophy, the Uhuru Cup, by Jomo Kenyatta when our imported Sea Port won. We had had him brought from England for this important race. He was a magnificent horse with paces as smooth as silence, legs as sound as steel hinges. Tom and I spent many happy occasions at the races. We had the luxury of the Delamere box at the Nairobi Racecourse. It is at the north end of the member's stand, in a prime position opposite the finishing post. Tom and I were leading owners for many years, and Diana Black, our trainer, was leading trainer. Tom's racing colours were brown and cream, and mine were pink and green. I had toyed with the idea of having Beryl Markham train some of our horses, but when I approached her, she was very cool, and I decided it wasn't worth the effort.

I spent a lot of time with the horses, watching them train and discussing their diets with the staff we employed. Tom was always a gambler, it was one of his passions, or perhaps one could say his bad habits. It did remind me a little of Jock, who had been an appallingly unlucky gambler, and even more so my father, but with Tom, I was tolerant. There was not much about him that I did not love. In return, he adored me, and I bathed in that delightful feeling.

Racing as it had been in Kenya before Independence was a much smaller affair. The exit of so many Europeans meant that most of the action was carried on mainly in Nairobi. To pursue our passion Tom and I travelled to England and spent a lot of time there in the racing world. We had the best trainers of the time, Sam Hall and Bernard van Cutsem. Lester Piggott was our favourite jockey.

Tom had long bouts of ill health, and I spent a lot of time fussing over him. I don't say this to try and present myself in a good light. It was just the way it was. I think in my old age, I stopped being so self-involved. I tried to care for the few people who had been good to me. Then, I would escape to the coast to go fishing. The captain of my boat was David Partridge, who was also the assistant manager of the Mnarani Club. My boat, named the Silver Bear, was the envy of all the other fishing people. She was thirty-eight feet long, twelve feet across and had a draught of two feet ten inches, with blue and white upholstery and blue carpet. Best of all, she had a flying bridge with full alternative controls. Patricia Fairweather used to come out with me, and we had so many successful days fishing the length of the Kenyan coastline, from north of Lamu to Shimoni in the south.

There were other noticeable changes in our lives. Once upon a time, we had employed male servants. Now female servants have become popular. It had begun with ayahs to look after the young children. The middle-class families in the cities were hiring female *dhobis* (laundry workers) and even female *mpishis* (cooks). The *shamba* was the worker who did the outside work. I didn't try and resist these changes. There was no point crying out for the past. I was realistic and pragmatic.

In 1968 I had a mild heart attack, which turned into angina. i couldn't live at the altitude of Soysambu for more than a month at a time. I was annoyed that ill-health forced me to leave Soysambu. I had spent a lot of time and money on improvements, and it was now a property with a certain quality of grandeur. I had overseen the landscaping of the gardens since I had arrived, and then I had a swimming pool installed, complete with a delightful gazebo where one could change and shower. I chose Spanish tiles and had arches built in various places as a token nod towards the architecture of Oserian. There was a darling tiered wedding-cake fountain. Tom and I had a charmed life at that stage, except for our ill health. We each had a new Mercedes every year, and we could indulge ourselves in any direction that we chose.

In 1974 we went on a Mediterranean cruise with our friend Marcus Wickham-Boynton. On that visit we attended the Royal London Yacht Club ball and went salmon fishing in Scotland. As Lady Delamere, I had become an acceptable member of the upper classes. I had always hoped that I would leave behind my notoriety as the lover of the murdered Lord Erroll, but that scandalous story lingered and probably would long after my death.

I was proud of Tom's contribution during those first years of Independence. He had worked with the new government and tried his best to help shape a new Kenya, doing what he could to get the best deal for the settlers and the new landowners. He was very generous when it came to his workers; they all received free healthcare and good quality housing and water supplies. They were well-fed, and Tom ensured each child received an education suitable for their talents. He certainly trimmed our landholdings and gave a lot of land away to his own employees for token prices. Unlike me, he was not ostentatious in his dress. I continued to wear the latest fashions and spent hours choosing which of my jewellery pieces to wear for every occasion when I deemed it suitable.

It seemed that many of the famous, eccentric, adventurous and aristocratic old settlers were dying in those days. Their children had grown up in Kenya to continue on the work but so often the land had been sold and they were the lost generation. Raymond Hook's wife, Joan was murdered in her house in 1968. The attacker was never identified. Margaret Elkington, daughter of the famous first-settler Jim Elkington, died in the ramshackle old colonial house, surrounded by her beloved dachshunds and cats, in 1976, aged 81 years.

What I found strange was that after Jock's trial, June Carberry never spoke to me again. Perhaps, it was for the best. Our dastardly secret did not slip out even in private conversations. I couldn't imagine her getting on with Gilbert. She was so shallow and silly. I supposed our friendship had been only for that time in my life, as I transitioned from a shallow blonde almost beauty into a woman who had experienced the depths of happiness and sadness and moved on with hard-won wisdom.

June's husband, JC, died in 1970, and the rumour was that as his demise occurred four days before the quarterly payment arrived, June put him in the freezer so that an obliging doctor would date the death certificate after the endowment was paid. Still shallow, spoiled and self-centred, June lived for another five years. She continued to drink and smoke heavily and lived in Johannesburg. She had always loved animals, and her obsession with dogs ruled her life. She would drive around the street in her chauffeur-driven car with another car behind her. She and her servants would pick up stray dogs, take them home, and care for them.

Jomo Kenyatta had ruled as President up until his death in 1978. Tom's first wife, Phyllis was dying of cancer in the late seventies, and Tom decreed that Hugh should not go and see her in her terrible state. He sent her a bottle of gin daily to help ease her pain.

Tom died of heart failure at Soysambu on Good Friday in 1979. He was buried at *Ndabibi* where Sarah and Gilbert were buried. His epitaph was '*So great a man*'. I was sixty-six years old. I had to quickly sell Tom's house in Mayfair as it was illegal to own property overseas. I decided that I would rent an apartment behind the Ritz Hotel in London and went and stayed there for several months every year.

I also spent much time at the coast, at Villa Buzza. I loved Kilifi, especially down at the jetty where there were cashew-nut peddlers. The smell was an intoxicating mixture of seaweed, mango, dried fish, coconut oil, ripe banana, jasmine, sandalwood, sweat and smoke. There was always a colourful crowd of fishermen, children and broad-hipped Giriama women dressed in bright *kangas*, balancing baskets on their heads. The beach was a mixture of coral rocks and fine white sand strewn with sea-bleached driftwood. Salty winds swirled around the silver baobabs. Mohammed, the barman at the Mnarani Club, could remember everyone's drink even though he was a Muslim and never drank himself. I would present the Lady Delamere Cup. All the boats would assemble to depart at sunrise, following the dream of sailfish, marlin, tuna or shark. They would sail back to shore with their brightly coloured flags flapping in the breeze to see who had got the biggest catch. Everyone drank Pims as the fish were weighed and the numbers plotted on an old blackboard.

I continued to go out on my boat and fish. It was one of the greatest passions in my life. There was something about being out on the sea that filled me with peace, and at the same time exhilaration. There was also that competitive element that was such a big part of my enjoyment of sports. I entered and won a great many fishing competitions.

Chapter Seventeen – The Twilight Years

For many of us, the 1980s saw everything falling apart in Kenya. The national population had increased exponentially. If you drove through Nairobi, the streets were thronged with an ocean of humanity. The variety of people encompassed many social groups, from neatly dressed office workers carrying briefcases, older women dressed in the traditional *kitenge* with bundles of sticks on their backs secured with leather straps across their foreheads, tribesmen in brightly coloured *shukas* herding cows with sticks, young men on bicycles, ramshackle pollution-belching cars, chauffeur-driven Mercedes full of rich black men and women, speeding buses packed with people, bundles strapped precariously on the roof. Endless houses and shacks made of flattened tin jerry cans sprawled across the Nairobi conurbation to house this vast sea of diverse humanity.

Throughout Kenya, land was still the major issue constantly disputed. Herdsmen in the Laikipia region were organised into armed militia groups and threatened the large landowners. They began with raids and invading pasture lands with their own herds of cattle.

The golden years of prosperity at Soysambu were over. I decided to sell *Ndabibi,* my property at Naivasha, to the Agricultural Development Corporation (ADC), a government parastatal established to facilitate the land transfer programme from settlers to Africans. I was given permission to take the money out of Kenya. When we cleaned out the house, I found some of Joss's belongings stored in the basement. I couldn't believe that I hadn't found them before. All the antique furniture was sent to auction.

In August 1981, Beryl Markham's cottage at Nairobi Racecourse was robbed. Her servant, Odero, slept a little distance away from her cottage in his own quarters and was surprised when he went to her door that morning to make her breakfast. She had not gotten up and unlocked her door, as was her usual custom. Eventually, he went and got help, and the local veterinarian broke in to find her bound with telephone cord, so tightly that her hands and feet had become horrendously swollen, and the circulation had stopped. She had been badly beaten and had bruising and cuts on her face and neck, and was virtually naked. Everything had been stolen, including her passport and driving licence.

By all reports that experience aged her a great deal. She walked stiffly. She had lost that lovely elegant lope for which she was famous. I used to see her at the Muthaiga Club, and sometimes we would exchange courtesies. In spite of my best attempts, she made it clear that she did not wish to be a friend of mine, and I found this very disappointing. I had heard so many accounts of her dazzling charm, but none was to be bestowed on me. She was a living legend, as they say, I was. Perhaps two living legends do not mix.

In 1982, shortly before the twentieth anniversary of Independence Day, there was an unsuccessful military coup. As befits a 'living legend' like Beryl, she got mixed up in it. She was driving to Muthaiga for Sunday lunch in her Mercedes and was stopped at a roadblock. The soldiers tried to search her car, and she accelerated and drove through the barrier. The soldiers opened fire at the car, and one bullet grazed her chin. She arrived at the club with blood smeared across her face, dripping from her chin, and her clothes badly blood stained. They say that these two experiences left their mark on her.

However, at that time, her novel *West With The Night* was republished and was received with great acclaim. There were many rumours that she had not written the book and that it might have been authored by her third husband, Raoul Schumacher. Then, the suggestion was put forward that the famous aviator and writer Saint-Exupéry had influenced her writing in the early days before she met Raoul, and certainly, she writes with something of his style.

I was sad when I heard that she had died on 3rd September 1986. She had fractured her hip, and after the operation, she seemed to be recovering well when she contracted pneumonia and died two days later. Her death was one day before the fiftieth anniversary of her record-breaking solo flight across the Atlantic. I read about a Thanksgiving service that they held at St Clements Dane church in London. This was a beautiful Wren church, and huge wreaths of white chrysanthemums were tied with ribbons of her racing colours.

In her last years, she had been utterly penniless, as she had been most of her life, and had relied on the charity of friends who contributed to an allowance. I must admit that my own financial position was muddled. It wasn't that I was penniless, far from it. Tom and I had sent a great deal of money overseas at the time of Independence. Somehow, I had lost track of it. One of the issues was mistrust of authorities and also individuals, and there were numerous trusts that had been created that I couldn't quite remember. On many occasions, I had had wills drawn up and then they had been discarded unsigned. On one level, I just couldn't face the fact of my inevitable death. I had struggled so hard to live and had survived in a world that seemed to have set its face against me. I let the harsh financial realities recede, and more and more, I lived in a dream world of reliving the past.

Beryl had died before me, but I knew that I was teetering on the edge. The Great Beyond was beckoning me. I had never clocked up any record feats, as Beryl had, although I had been cherished by two wonderful men, Gilbert and Tom, and I had my daughter Snoo with whom I had always had a good relationship. This was more than Beryl, who seemed unable to forge meaningful conjugal and familial relationships. I had lived in luxury with almost unlimited wealth since 1943 when I married Gilbert, while Beryl had been constantly broke and often relied on her friends for money just to survive. Perhaps Beryl could have come up with an interesting intellectual comment on the differences in our lives, but I did not have the wit.

In 1981 James Fox, who was still writing *White Mischief*, knocked on my door in London. An account of our meeting is included in the penultimate chapter of his book. I told him to return in a week, and we had a couple of long and interesting conversations before the book was published.

I found some of his observations very interesting, and I will re-tell them here as food for thought. He said that the fact that I commented on the cold in London reminded him of the way in which Antonia Fraser said that Mary Queen of Scots and Diana Delamere suffered from the chill of being *femmes fatales*. It could be that I lived most of my life in Kenya, which has a very warm climate compared to dull, grey England.

I was relieved that he did not judge me 'cold' or 'hard', which were characteristics attributed to me so often and tirelessly. He quoted Cyril Conolly who had said that I had 'a talent for enjoyment and bringing out enjoyment in others.'

Mr Fox had misrepresented himself. He said that he wanted to write about Erroll in the context of what it revealed about Kenya, with Broughton as an interesting central character, not to 'rehash an old scandal'. This was a big fat lie! His whole book was about rehashing the scandal. He had the grace to record that I told him I didn't do it.

I implied that it might well have been Jock who had done it. This was what I had believed for quite some time, that he had arranged it with a black assassin, and it was easy to fall in with the line that this journalist seemed to be taking. When he questioned me more closely about the events of that night, whether or not I had heard Jock coming back into the house, I wheeled out the old excuse of my mind shutting down when it came to past traumatic events. Of course, I hadn't heard Jock coming back in, I was out in the night fleeing for my life, then lying in bed with June having been shot!

I did tell him the story of how Joss had wanted me to come in the French doors. This was true and served as a useful red herring, but at the time, I had thought that it was merely

Jock trying to exercise a pathetically small piece of tyrannical power over me. I told him the truth about going on safari that I was afraid of Joss, who was behaving very strangely.

The trickiest part of one of the conversations was whether or not Joss and I had had a row at the end of that fateful evening. I point-blank denied it, saying that it was my eternal regret that Joss and I had never got down to reality. We had never argued. This was, of course, totally untrue! Then, we went into the kitchen, and I busied myself preparing snacks.

When I read his book, I found that Wilkie had been interviewed in Durban, South Africa. She said that I had come in that night with a 'face like thunder', went upstairs and then came down again. She had stayed in June's room talking to her and had not heard Joss's car driving away. She said she heard me coming back upstairs about half an hour later and that June and I had been talking excitedly for some time. I am sure that I was away watching Joss being murdered and running home for more than half an hour. Wilkie had told the truth, but she hadn't appeared as a witness at the trial. What was interesting was her admiration of Jock. I think she must have been the only person in the world who saw any good in the odious old man.

Mr Fox said I would take my secrets to the grave, 'leaving a tantalising tale untold'. In my experience, the older we get, the more easily the glib lies slip off our tongue. The idea of setting the record straight before we died, like spies telling state secrets on their death beds, is exaggerated. In this writing, I have endeavoured to tell the truth, but the habits of a lifetime are hard to break.

Since 1982, I have been sick. But, nothing as dramatic as Beryl being robbed and beaten, shot during a coup or fracturing a hip. I spent most days lying in the summerhouse of my house on the north side of the creek at Kilifi. I had a luxurious four-poster bed surrounded by couches and easy chairs and the room was filled with potted plants. I could lie in my bed there, propped up by many silk pillows and cushions. I had had my huge collection of teddy bears moved into the room with me. I had always had a penchant for teddy bears. I remembered one Christmas, the owner of the Nairobi toyshop, sent up his whole collection of bears, and I asked my little grandson to choose. He had selected a large white one. I did approve of that choice.

I loved my house at Kilifi, surrounded by manicured lawns stretching down to the water. Exotic palms were planted amongst tall whispering trees. No matter whether alone or expecting visitors, I made sure that my hair was coiffed and my makeup perfect. For so long, I had been practising the art of a living legend, wrapped in myth and mystery that I knew no other way of being. I liked to wear flowing chiffon gowns. I had moved away from the very tailored couture of Hardy Aimes and chose clothes that were more comfortable but still flawlessly elegant.

I spent every year migrating between Nairobi and the racecourse, or Kilifi and boating. I still managed to go out on my boat, the *White Bear,* with flags flying. I never lost my love of deep-sea fishing.

I loved to socialise and indulged in talking with the old people about former times at Muthaiga Club, race days and glorious victories of favourite horses, and fishing days when the marlin had leapt onto our hooks.

I spent some time engaged in introspection, and it did seem that I had found my own niche in history. I humoured myself with the belief that stories about me were in the same class as those about Karen Blixen and Ernest Hemingway. Most of this was probably due to my role as the *'femme fatale'* in the affair of Joss's murder. I could do nothing to stop the inevitable stories that became more fantastic over the years. I continued to dress immaculately and never hid my wealth, but I did not display it in a manner that could be considered distasteful. In later life, my presence and deportment were often reported as regal. I presented the Lady Delamere Cup for an annual fishing competition. I had played this role for so long that it was now an indelible part of my behaviour.

I had gone to Africa to find freedom in a bright, sunshine-filled existence, and along the way Africa had imprinted itself upon my soul. I think it was from Gilbert that I discovered a love of the essence of this great land. I created for myself a version of African existence that survived the tumult of Independence.

I never did get into that fashionable activity of saving the wildlife. I had gone shooting on safari and had famously even shot a lion on that safari after Joss was killed. I loved horses and dogs, or at least specific horses and particular dogs. According to Beryl these noble creatures are not dumb, nor loyal, but merely tolerant. She went on to say that if she did not have the care of one of these animals, she would be as 'concerned as a Buddhist monk, having lost contact with Nirvana.' But I wasn't really an animal person. Certainly not like Alice de Trafford, who was famously photographed with a huge lion cub on her lap, nor June who spent her last years searching the streets for stray dogs. While others turned to creating reserves for wildlife, I lived at the coast and went fishing.

Life leaps from the cosmic to the mundane. I spend time wondering about the meaning of my life and the lives of other women who I have admired. Then a household disaster springs up where no one can locate my pills for my heart condition. My staff rush around in a flurry, and I wonder whether I will gasp my last because the pill bottle has rolled under a large piece of furniture and remains undiscovered until it is too late. The ghosts of my past rattle around my present.

Diana Mosley was still alive. Her husband, the redoubtable Oswald, Tom to his friends, died in December 1980 and they were together until the end. She was faithful to him and his doctrines even, or perhaps more so, after his death. Perhaps, Diana could not face the truth that her own life had been blighted with prison at the time that two of her boys were babies, and the lifelong social ostracism that she had suffered. She had to maintain a justification for all that had happened to her. She had developed a special talent for seeing what she wanted to see. She was such an intelligent and elegant woman but seemed to have a blind spot a mile wide. She adored her husband Tom and would brook no criticism of him. She acknowledged he was a philanderer, but this was outweighed by the fact of his brilliance. She also maintained her admiration of Hitler. Such views were not acceptable in her time, nor perhaps at any time, but she clung to them. Perhaps she had to continue to believe, or else the basis and rationale of her life would be rendered ridiculous without them. Her stalwart defence of Mosley was certainly a feat of strength and endurance.

She lived in a beautiful house called the Temple in a small village, Orsay, twenty miles from Paris. Apparently, it was a classic temple in miniature. It had the Palladian façade of a Greco-Roman temple with four Corinthian columns rising from the first-floor balcony to the roof. I did wonder whether I shouldn't have tried to have such a magnificent and distinctive architect-designed house built for me in Kenya. Still, ultimately, I decided to continue to enjoy the comfort and luxury of my own houses. It wasn't wise to display wealth ostentatiously in Kenya.

Mary, Tom's second wife, died in October 1986. Even after they divorced, she had insisted that she had the sole claim on the title of Lady Delamere, a claim which I refused to countenance. She never forgave me for stealing her husband. Now, there was no argument. I was irrefutably Lady Delamere. She was certainly never one of the women who I had admired. There was no sense of greatness or style about her at all. Her elder sister, Edwina, had been a very flawed, but able and interesting woman. Mary had drip-fed dollops of malicious gossip and slander about her sister over the years after she had died, and for that, no one could admire her.

I did indulge in what the psychologists call 'counter-factual thinking', what might have happened if something else had happened. I pondered what might have happened if Joss had lived and I had become the Countess of Erroll. We would have travelled to Europe after the war and been intimate with the Mosleys and the Windsors. It was a life in which I would have struggled to keep up a front of intellectuality and wit. Being Gilbert's wife and then Lady Delamere in Kenya had been achievable, and I believed I had made a success of it.

I have to set the record straight on one other issue. I was often lumped in with the hedonistic Happy Valley people, unkindly described as a coterie of louche layabouts who were considered a disgrace to the more moral and hard-working white settlers. I never lived in Wanjohi Valley, which was the geographical location of Happy Valley. The only member of that group who had ever accepted me was Joss. Idina and Alice, the *grandes dames* had in the early days a hardened dislike of me. Idina might have given me an audience on that fateful afternoon when I talked to her about Joss's death, but I was never a part of that coterie, nor was Gilbert or Tom. The murder of Joss did bring about the end of those Happy Valley days, but at that stage, he had left those times behind him when he had moved down to Nairobi and thrown himself into war work and a political career.

I have sometimes wondered how Joss would have survived Independence. He would have been sixty-three years old when the British flag was lowered for the last time. He had been firmly of the opinion that the white settlers should rule Kenya. Would he have changed his view and acknowledged that the black Africans had a right to the land that had been taken from them? I'm not sure he would have been able to embrace the new order and find himself a position within it. We will never know.

Diana, Lady Delamere died in 1987, aged 74 years,

in London.

Her body was flown back to Kenya

and she was buried at *Ndabibi*,

between the graves of Gilbert and Tom.

"Surrounded by all I love".

Bibliography

Arlen, Michael, *The Green Hat,* published 1924 by Collins, London.

Barnes, Juliet, *For Love of Soysambu: The Saga of Lord Delamere and his Descendants in Kenya,* published 2020, Old African Books, Naivasha, Kenya.

Barnes, Juliet, *The Ghosts of Happy Valley: Searching For The Lost World of Africa's Infamous Aristocrats,* published 2013 by Aurum Press Ltd, London.

Best, Nicholas, *Happy Valley: The Story of the English in Kenya*, published 2013, Martin, Secker, Warburg.

Blixen, Karen (Isak Dinesen), *Out of Africa,* published 1937, republished 1954 by Penguin Books, London.

Carberry, Juanita, with Tyrer, Nicola, *Child of Happy Valley: A Memoir*, published 1999 by William Heinemann, London.

Coutts, Chryso, *Are You Married, or Do You Live in Kenya,* published 2019.

De Courcy, Anne, *Diana Mosley,* published 2003 by Chatto and Windus, London.

De Janzé, Frédéric, *Vertical Land,* published 1928 by Duckworth, London, republished by Epona Publishing.

De Marigny, Alfred, and Herskowitz, Mickey, *A Conspiracy of Crowns: The Murder Case of the 20th Century*, published by Garret County Press, New Orleans.

Fox, James, *White Mischief,* published 1982 by Jonathan Cape, UK.

Gallman, Kuki, *I Dreamed of Africa,* published 1991 by Viking.

Gallman, Kuki, *African Nights,* published 1994 by Penguin Books, London.

Hornsby, Charles, *Kenya: A History Since Independence,* published by I.B.Taurus.

Huxley, Elspeth, *The Flame Trees of Thika: Memories of an African Childhood,* published 1959 by Chatto and Windus, London.

Huxley, Elspeth, *Out In The Midday Sun,* published 1985, republished 2000 by Pimlico, London.

Lovell, Mary S., *Straight on till Morning,* first published 1987, republished by Hachette Digital, London.

Lovell, Mary S., *The Riviera Set,* published 2016 by Little Brown, London.

Lownie, Andrew, *The Mountbattens: Their Lives and Loves,* published 2019 by Blink Publishing, London.

Markham, Beryl, *West With The Night,* published 1942, republished 1984 by Virago Press, London.

Mitford, Nancy, *The Pursuit of Love,* published 1945 by Penguin Books, London.

Osborne, Frances, *The Bolter,* published 2008, by Hachette Digital, London.

Spicer, Paul, *The Temptress: Passion And Murder in Kenya's Happy Valley,* published 2010 by Simon and Schuster, UK Ltd

Topps, Tim, *The Umzindusi Letter: Does this solve the Lord Erroll murder?,* published 2017 by Matador, Leicestershire.

Trzebinski, Errol, *The Life and Death of Lord Erroll: The Truth Behind The Happy Valley Murder,* published 2001 by The Fourth Estate Ltd, London.

Printed in Great Britain
by Amazon